U0060306

世界文學台讀少年雙語系列 ②

青瓦厝ê安妮

(台英雙語‧附台語朗讀)

原著｜Lucy Maud Montgomery
主編｜陳麗君
台譯｜黃昭瑞、白麗芬
插畫｜Asta Wu

序一
幸福 ê 向望

「你 ê 英語 m̄ 是 tsiok láu？你哪會無 kap in 講英語？」若知影我是英文老師 suah kap ka-kī ê gín-á 講台語，真 tsē 人會 án-ne 問我。

Tī 解嚴時代尾期大漢，華語是我過去主要 ê 語言。一直到十二冬前有身 ê 時，我開始思考，我 ê gín-á ê 母語／爸語應該是啥。翁婿 ê 母語是英語，所以伊當然 kap gín-á 講英語。雖然台語是我 ê 母語，m̄-koh 因為 sionn 久無講，我對 ka-kī li-li-lak-lak ê 台語真無把握。

佳哉有翁婿 ê 支持 kap ka-kī ê 堅持，我慢慢 á 一字一句 kap 阮 kiánn 講台語，hit 陣台語 ê 資源比 tsit-má khah 少，我 ài kā 華語 kap 英語 ê gín-á 冊翻做台語講 hōo in 聽，mā 因為 án-ne，我 kā 台語 koh khioh 轉來。Gín-á khah 大漢了後，gín-á 冊已經無夠 thang 用 ah，我才發現市面上無寫 hōo 少年 gín-á ê 故事冊，真 tú 好麗君教授招我來參與「世界文學台讀少年雙語讀物」ê 計畫。

我選《安妮》是因為我真佮意 tsit 本冊 kap 安妮 tsit 个主角，伊 hōo 我想 tiȯh 阮查某 kiánn 阿晴，活潑 koh 堅強；伊 ê 想像力 kap 同理心 mā 親像阮大漢 kiánn 阿源。Kap 咱每一人 kâng 款，安妮向望有歸屬感，伊透過 thut-tshuê 來學 tiȯh 經驗，伊 tshuē-tiȯh 愛 mā 失去愛。

百 guā 冬前加拿大 ê 孤女 hōo 一對無嫁娶 ê 兄妹 á 收養 ê 成長故事，tī tsit-má 進步 ê 台灣社會來看 iu-guân 對同，因爲血統 m̄ 是圓滿家庭上重要 ê 元素，是愛、差異、了解、接受 kap 故事來組成全世界 ê 多元家庭。

黃昭瑞 N̂g Tsiau-suī

譯者

序二
守護台灣，疼惜台文

　　人講：拍鐵 tiȯh-ài suà 火！阮十二萬分歡喜，tī《你無聽--過 ê 格林童話》tsiah tú 出版 iáu 無半冬 ê tsit tang 陣，由「天母扶輪社福爾摩沙委員會」贊助國立成功大學陳麗君教授團隊所編譯 ê《青瓦厝 ê 安妮》mā teh-beh 出版 ah。

　　「天母扶輪社」對台灣文化 ê 支持，一向就親像台灣人「做牛無惜力」ê 精神盡心盡力。眞 tú 好，今年是咱「天母社」成立四十週年慶，阮當然 ài 特別加插預算，hōo tsit 个美麗 ê tú-tīng koh khah 圓滿，更加向望 thìng 好爲推 sak 台語文 tsit 塊田地 iā kuá 肥塗。

　　現此時，眞 tsē 少年人，就算講伊自細漢 kah 厝內 ê 序大長輩 lóng 用台語做日常 ê 溝通，m̄-koh，有法度講 kah 眞 lián 轉 ê tsiânn 少。M̄-nā án-ne，就連咱不時 to 聽會 tiȯh ê 俗諺語，in mā 像「鴨 á 聽雷」，tsia--ê lóng 是台灣先祖 ê 智慧 neh！看 tiȯh tsit 款現象，hōo 阮對台語文 ê 傳承有影心 tsiânn 憂。

　　佳哉！透過 tsit 一系列 ê 台語童話編譯，看 tiȯh 咱前社長翁肇喜先生，長久以來對台灣文化 ê 注心 kah 堅持，確實使人欽佩。加上「福爾摩沙委員會」主委前社長溫宏義先生以及 tsē-tsē 社友資源 ê 投入 kah sio-thīn，tī 陳麗君教授團隊和齊 phah-piànn 之下，咱 tsit 本英譯台 ê《青瓦厝

ê 安妮》才會得順利出版。希望各界資源 ē-tàng sann-kap sio-kīng，有 koh khah tsē 社會 ê 賢達，願意加入「守護台灣，疼惜台文」ê 事工，藉阮輕 báng ê tsit-sut-á 心力，發揮「tàn 石討玉」ê 能量，piak 出上光焱 ê 火金星，hōo ták-ke 見證咱台灣社會 ê 性命力！

侯舒文 Philip

台北天母扶輪社第四十屆（2021-2022）社長

序三

Khiā 台灣，看世界！

21 世紀後疫情時代，台灣 ê 優等表現得 tiȯh 國際上 bē 少支持 kap 肯定。台灣認同覺醒，hōo 咱 khiā 起 tī 世界舞台 kap 全球競合。Suà 落來，ài án-tsuánn 掌握時世展現 Taiwan can help ê 能量 leh？個人認爲發展「全球在地化」（Glocalization）ê 思維 hām 行動，推動「在地全球化」（Logloblization）ê 行銷 kài 重要。以 tsit 款思考 ê 理路來應用 tiàm 教育發展，mā 一定是落實教育 ê 子午針。

咱 tsit 套「世界文學台讀少年雙語系列」讀物是爲 tiȯh beh 建立青少年對「在地主體 ê 認同」以及 hùn 闊「世界觀」雙向 ê 目標，按算 thai 選「英美、日、德、法、俄、越南」等國 ê 名著，進行「忠於經典原文 ê 台文翻譯 kap 轉寫」，做雙語 (台語／原文)ê 編輯發行。向望透過 tsit 套冊 kap-uá 世界文學，推廣咱 ê 台語，落實語文教育 kap 閱讀 ê 底蒂。透過本土語文閱讀世界，認 bat 文化文學，才有法度翻頭轉來建立咱青少年對自我、台灣土地 ê 認同。Tī 議題 ê 揀選，爲 beh 配合《國家語言發展法》，融入 12 年課綱 ê 題材，mā 要意聯合國永續性發展目標 （Sustainable Develpoment Goals, SDGs），親像性平教育、人權教育、環境教育等議題，會使提供多元題材，發展全人教育 ê 世界觀。台語文字 （漢羅 thàu-lām） koh 加上優質配音，眞適合自學 hām 親子共讀。

「語言是民族 ê 靈魂、mā 是文化 ê 載體」，眞知影「本土語文青少年讀物」tī 質 hām 量是 tsiah-nī 欠缺，本人 tī 2017 年 4 月 hit 當時開始寫 tsit 份「台語世界文學兒童雙語閱讀計畫」beh 出版。是講哪有 tsiah 容易？Kíann beh 生會順序，mā ài 有產婆！咱台灣雖罔有 70% 以上 ê 族群人口使用台語，kâng 款 mā 是 tshun 氣絲 á 喘 leh 喘 leh，強欲 hua 去，因爲有心 beh 推 sak 抑是發心 beh 贊助 ê 專門機構眞少。哪會知影 3 年後 2020 年 ê 開春，翁肇喜社長引領扶輪社「福爾摩沙委員會」ê 要員，對台北專工來到台南開會，開講 tioh「台灣語文教育 ê 未來發展」ê 議論，因爲 tsit 个機緣，tsiáng 時 tsit 套有聲冊才有 thang 出世。

幼嬰 á 出世麻油芳，事工 beh 圓滿 mā ài 感謝咱上有本土心本土味 ê 前衛出版社提供印刷 ê 協助，本團隊無分國籍所有 ê 雙語文翻譯、潤稿校稿 ê 老師，以及錄音團隊共同努力所成就 ê。我相信 suà 落來 ê 水波效應所反射出來 ê 魚鱗光，絕對 m̄-nā 是 kan-na 帶動台語文冊 ê 出版，更加是台灣本土語文 ê 新生 kap 再生！

陳麗君

國立成功大學台灣文學系教授

「世界文學台讀少年雙語系列」企劃主編

目次

Contents

第一章
起頭

　　燒熱 ê 六月天 e-poo，藺太太（Mrs. Lynde）倚去灶跤 ê 窗 á 外看外口，無疑悟去看 tiòh 高馬修（Mathew Cuthbert）開馬車經過。

　　藺太太心內想講：「馬修 ê 個性 tsiânn pì-sù，罕得 kah 別人 leh sio-kau-tshap，是 án-tsuánn 今 á 日穿 kah tsiah-nī pih-tsah 出門？伊是 beh 去 tó 位？我 tiòh 來 kā 了解一下。」

　　藺太太上愛 tshap 亞檬里（Avonlea）內底所有大大細細 ê 代誌，伊想 tiòh 高馬修 kah 伊 ê 小妹高瑪俐

（Marilla Cuthbert）同齊 tuà tī 庄內 ê 青瓦厝，隨就 tsáu 去 in tau。

Tng 藺太太踏入去青瓦厝 ê 時，瑪俐 tú 好 tī 灶跤 leh 無閒，伊生做瘦抽瘦抽，已經 tām-pȯh-á 轉 phú 白 ê 烏頭毛捲 ân-ân pȧk tī 後 khok。

瑪俐講：「麗秋姊（Rachael），請坐，e-poo 哪有閒來 tshuē 我？」

藺太太講：「我看馬修 tú-á 出去，驚講 kám 是你人無爽快，伊才趕緊 beh 去請醫生來 kā 你看。」

瑪俐講：「無啦！我人無 án-tsuánn 啦！是因爲阮 uì 勞碼社（Nova Scotia）ê 孤兒院 tshíng-tiȯh 一個查埔 gín-á，tsit 个 gín-á e-poo 會坐火車到咱 tsia，所以阮阿兄是 beh 去明河車頭（Bright River）接伊啦！」

藺太太聽 tiȯh 驚一 tiô，心肝內想講，in 兄妹 á 竟然 beh pun 一个查埔 gín-á 來 iúnn！這眞正是三斤貓咬四斤 niáu 鼠 ê hàm 古。伊就 kā 瑪俐講：「啥物？你是 leh 講 sńg 笑 hiooh？」

瑪俐講：「無啊！我 kám 是會烏白亂講 ê 人？阮大兄有歲 ah，體力無 khah 早 hiah-nī 好，伊需要一个查埔 gín-á tī 農場 kā 伊 tàu 跤手。」

雖然藺太太 tsiok 想 beh 留落來等馬修 tshuā hit 个查埔 gín-á 來，m̄-koh án-ne 伊 tiòh-ài 等候兩點 guā 鐘久，所以伊按算先去 tshuē 隔壁 ê 馬太太（Mrs. Bell），kā 伊報 tsit 个天大地大 ê 消息。藺太太 ná kiânn ná 想：「Hit 个孤兒若 beh 來 tuè 馬修 kah 瑪俐，就實在真無 siá-sì，in 兩个兄妹 á 根本 to bē-hiáu 飼 gín-á。」

　　馬修到車站 ê 時無看 tiòh 火車，kan-na 看 tiòh 長 lò-lò ê 月台盡尾，有一个查某 gín-á 坐 tī hia。

　　車站 ê 站長 tú 好 leh 鎖賣票間 á，馬修就問伊：「請問五點半 hit 幫車 tang 時會到站？」

　　站長講：「Hit 幫車早就過 ah，有一个查某 gín-á 落車講 beh tshuē 你。」

　　馬修講：「M̄-tiòh 喔！應該是查埔 gín-á，m̄ 是查某 gín-á 喔！」

　　站長講：「抑無，你 kah 伊講看 māi，伊已經等 tsiok 久 ah。」

　　Tsit 个查某 gín-á 穿一領舊 àu 舊臭 ê 破洋裝，紅色 ê 長頭毛 pīnn 兩條油 tsiàh 粿，頂 kuân 戴一頂退色 ê 帽 á，面模 á 幼秀幼秀，有雀斑，兩蕊青 lin-lin ê 目睭 put-tsí-á 大蕊。

查某 gín-á 問馬修：「請問你 kám 是高馬修先生？我 tsiok 驚你無 beh 來 ah，本 tsiânn 按算講你若無來，我 e 暗就 beh peh-khí-lí hit 欉樹 á 頂睏，你 kám 有感覺睏 tī 月娘 tshiō kah 光 sih-sih ê 樹 á 頂是 tsiok 嬈、tsiok 浪漫 ê 代誌？」

　　馬修看 tsit 个查某 gín-á ê 眼神 tsiah-nī-á 熱誠，伊知影，頭起先是 beh tih 查埔 ê tsit 件代誌，伊是講 bē 出 tshuì ê，無論 án-tsuánn 伊 ing 暗 lóng tio̍h-ài 先 tshuā tsit 个查某 gín-á 轉去厝裡。「歹勢，我 tsiah-nī uànn 才到。來！你 ê 袋 á hōo 我 kuānn。」

查某 gín-á 講：「我 ka-kī kuānn 就好啦！雖然我所有 ê 家伙 lóng tī 內底，m̄-koh bē kài 重。」

馬修牽伊 tsiūnn 馬車了後，伊開始講：「我 tsiok 歡喜 ē-tàng kah 你 tuà 做伙！你 kám bat tuà 過孤兒院？Hia 是全世界上無聊 ê 所在，因爲 tī hia，完全無法度發揮咱 ê 想像力，無白賊！」查某 gín-á tsiū-án-ne 沿路直直講、直直講，講 kah 轉去到亞檬里，馬修 mā 聽 kah 耳 á phak-phak，感覺伊 tsiânn 古錐。

In 開過一粒山 koh sèh 過一个 uat 角，遠遠 ê 山跤有一 kuá 農舍，查某 gín-á 手 kí 其中一間，問講：「Hit 間 kám 是恁 ê 青瓦厝？」

馬修 tìm 頭：「無 m̄-tiòh，就是 hit 間。」

查某 gín-á 歡喜 kah tshuì 笑目笑 koh 吐一个大氣講：「我本來 tsiok 驚是 leh hām 眠，m̄-koh 是眞 ê！是眞 ê！咱已經到厝 ah！」

第二章
錯誤

In 轉來到青瓦厝 ah。馬修一下開門,瑪俐就 kiânn 出來。瑪俐看 tiȯh hit 个查某 gín-á,驚一 tiô,問馬修:「阿兄,tsit 个 gín-á 是 siáng？查埔 gín-á leh？」

馬修講:「無查埔 gín-á,kan-na 伊 niā。」

瑪俐講:「咱是 beh ài 查埔 gín-á neh！」

馬修講:「In 就是 hōo 咱查某 gín-á,我只好先 tshuā 伊 tò 轉來,án-tsuánn 講 mā bē-tàng kā 伊留 tiàm 車頭啊！」

「原來恁 buaih tih 我！」查某 gín-á koh 講：「我早就應該知影這一切 lóng 是夢，哪有可能有人 beh 收留我？」講 suah，伊就坐 tiàm 椅 á 頂開始哭。

瑪俐講：「Aih-ioh……這 kám 有需要哭！」

查某 gín-á 愈哭愈傷心，目屎 sì-lâm-suî 講：「當然有需要！這是我 tsit 世人 tú 過上 kài 悽慘 ê 代誌。」

瑪俐險險 á 笑出來，伊講：「你先 mài 哭 ah。阮 ing 暗 bē 送你 tò 轉去啦！你叫啥物名？」

查某 gín-á tùn-tenn 一時 á，才 ìn 講：「你 kám ē-tàng 叫我柯蒂莉（Cordelia）？」

瑪俐感覺無對同，就問伊：「這 kám 真正是你 ê 名？」

查某 gín-á 承認講：「M̄……m̄ 是啦！我 ê 真名是施安（Anne Shirley），ták-ke lóng 叫我安 á，m̄-koh 我 khah 佮意柯蒂莉 tsit 個名，聽起來 ke 真浪漫 neh ！」

瑪俐講：「烏白講！安 á 明明就是一个好聽 ê 名。」

查某 gín-á 講：「你 nā beh 叫我安 á，kám ē-tàng kā『á』改做『妮』？我感覺『安妮』聽起來比『安 á』khah 親，mā khah 有氣質。」

瑪俐講：「好！好！好！是安妮 m̄ 是安 á。是講，安妮，你 kám ē-tàng kā 阮講是 án-tsuánn m̄ 是查埔 gín-á 來阮 tsia leh？」

安妮講：「史平雪（Spencer）太太 tsiok 確定講怹是 beh ài 一个大約十一歲 ê 查某 gín-á。阮孤兒院有一个 gín-á 叫做蔣俐俐（Lily Jones），因為伊生做真古錐，史平雪太太就 kā 伊留 tiàm 身軀邊做伴。瑪俐阿姨，假使我 mā 生做古錐款，怹 kám beh 收留我？」

瑪俐講：「Mā 是無法度。因為阮就是 beh ài 一个查埔 gín-á 來農場 tàu 跤手，阮無欠查某 gín-á。」

In 坐落來食暗頓，安妮 kan-na 食一兩 tshuì á niā-niā。

馬修 kā 瑪俐講：「伊 huān 勢 thiám ah，先 tshuā 伊去睏。」

瑪俐 tshuā 安妮去東 pîng ê 房間。Tsit 間房間細細間 á，內底真簡單，無啥物裝潢，kan-na tī 邊 á 角排一頂眠床，塗跤中央 tshu 一塊針織 ê 圓地毯 niā。安妮目屎 kâm 目 kînn ná 換一 su 退色 ê 睏衫了後，就跳 khí-lí 眠床頂，giú 棉 tsioh-phuē 來 kā 規身軀連頭 lóng khàm 起來。

瑪俐講：「好 ah，緊睏。」

Tsit 時安妮白 tshang-tshang ê 面 kah 大大蕊 ê 目睭 uì 被單下跤探出來講:「你哪 ē-tàng 叫我緊睏?你明明 to 知影 ing 暗是我 tsit 世人上悽慘 ê 一暝。」講 suah,伊 koh kā 頭 khàm 起來。

　　瑪俐 tò 轉去灶跤 kā in 大兄講:「咱一定 ài kā 伊送轉去孤兒院。」

　　馬修講:「M̄-koh 伊眞乖,若 kā 送轉去 tsiok 無彩,伊已經按算 beh kah 咱 tuà 做伙 ah。」

　　瑪俐氣 phut-phut 講:「你想 beh kā 伊留落來?一个查某 gín-á 是有才調 tàu 做啥?」

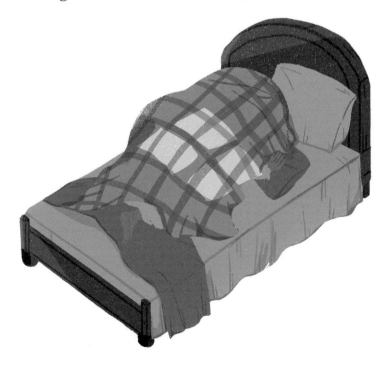

馬修講:「Kiám-tshái 咱會需要伊,koh 再講,伊 mā ē-tàng kah 你做伴啊!」

瑪俐講:「我免人做伴!我才無 ài kā 伊留落來。」

馬修講:「你發落就好,我 beh 來去睏 ah。」

瑪俐 kā 碗箸洗好、灶跤 khuán 好了後 mā 去睏 ah,tī 樓頂東 pîng 細間房間內底,有一个查某 gín-á m̄ 知哭 kah 幾點才睏去。

第三章
安妮 ê 過去

　　安妮睏醒了後，坐 tiàm 眠床頂，suah hiông-hiông m̄ 知影 ka-kī tsit 陣 tī tó 位？後來才想 tiòh 伊是 tī 青瓦厝，m̄-koh in buaih tih 伊，只因為伊是查某 gín-á。

　　安妮跳落眠床，跪 tī 塗跤看窗 á 外。厝 ê 雙 pîng 邊 á 是蘋果樹 kah 櫻桃樹，花園內面有茄 á 色花蕊開 kah 真 ōm ê 丁香樹，花園後壁有一片 tshu-tshu ê 草埔，順草埔 tshu 落去下底 hia 有一條溪，koh 過去是一粒 lóng 是種雲杉 kah 冷杉 ê 山崙。

無 tiunn-tî，一肢手來 tah tī 安妮 ê 肩胛頭，kā 伊 heh 驚 tiòh。

原來是瑪俐，伊 kā 安妮講：「你好 thang 換衫 ah。」

安妮 khiā 起來講：「Tsia ê 環境 tsiah-nī 媠，我 tú-tsiah 才 leh 想像我 teh-beh 永遠 tuà tī tsia⋯⋯」

瑪俐講：「你緊去換衫來食早頓，mài koh 烏白想 ah。」

過一時 á 安妮面洗清氣，頭毛 pīnn 兩條油 tsiàh 粿，穿 kah 真 pih-tsah，uì 樓頂 kiânn 落來樓跤。

早頓食飽，瑪俐問安妮：「你 kám ē-hiáu 洗碗？」

安妮講：「無問題啊！論真講，我 koh khah gâu 照顧 gín-á。是講，恁 tsia mā 無細漢 gín-á thang hōo 我顧，真無彩！」

瑪俐講：「我無需要 koh 再有別个 gín-á！Kan-na 你就真費氣 ah！我 tsit-má mā m̄ 知 beh án-tsuánn 發落你⋯⋯哎！這 lóng 是阮 hit 个 gōng 大兄 tì-ìm ê。」

安妮講：「伊真古錐 neh！我一下看 tiòh 伊，就知影阮兩个人會 tsiânn 做 mah-tsih。」

瑪俐講：「在我看 honnh，恁兩个 lóng 是怪跤。

你 tsit-má 去洗碗，ke 用 kuá 燒水洗，洗好 ài koh tshit hōo ta。」

碗洗了，瑪俐講安妮 ē-tàng 去外口 tshit-thô。

聽 tiȯh án-ne，安妮歡喜 kah kōo tsáu ê，tsáu 到門跤口 suah hiông-hiông tòng leh，uat 轉來坐 tī 灶跤 ê 食飯桌 tsia。

瑪俐講：「Tann 你是 koh án-tsuánn？」

安妮講：「我 m̄ 敢出去 tshit-thô，因爲我若出去一定會去愛 tiȯh 所有 ê 花、樹 á、果子園 kah 溪 á。我本來 mā tsiok 歡喜 teh-beh tuà tī tsia，ē-tàng tȧk 工看 tsia-ê 媠 ê 物件 koh kah in 做朋友，m̄-koh tsit-má 我 tsit 个美夢已經烏有去 ah，khah 看 mā 無 khah-tsuȧh，規氣 mài 出去，tiàm tsia 坐就好。」

安妮一直 tī hia 坐到馬修 tò 轉來食晝。食飯 ê 時瑪俐講：「我等 leh beh kā 安妮載去白沙鄉（White Sands）交 hōo 史平雪太太，伊應該會安排 kā 安妮送轉去孤兒院。」

馬修 tiām-tiām 無講話，食飯飽就去 kā 馬車 tshuân 好勢，koh kā 頭前埕 ê 門開--開，thang hōo 瑪俐 kah 安妮出去。瑪俐 uȧt 頭看馬修 phīng tī 門邊，眞傷心 ê 款。

安妮講：「我已經決定 beh 好好 á 享受 tsit tsuā 路，先 mài 去想孤兒院 ê 代誌，咱今 á 日會經過金爍湖 bô？」

瑪俐講：「你是講白家 ê 水池，是 bô？咱 beh kiânn 海坲 ê 路，bē 經過 hia。」

安妮講：「海 kînn ê 路聽起來眞浪漫，白沙 tsit 个地名 mā tsiok 好聽，m̄-koh 我上佮意亞檬里，講起來若親像 tī leh 唱歌！」

瑪俐講：「若準你 tsit 陣想 beh 話仙，就來講你 ka-kī ê 故事。」

安妮講：「我 tī 努琶司高社（Nova Scotia）出世，今年十二歲。阮阿爸是施亞濤（Walter Shirley），阿母叫做施琶莎（Bertha Shirley），in 以前 lóng 是學校 ê 老師。M̄-koh 我 iáu 是嬰 á ê 時，in 就過身 ah。因爲我無親 tsiânn thang 倚靠，beh án-tsuánn 處理我？Suah 無人 sa 有 tsáng。尾手是卓瑪舒（Thomas）太太收留我 ê。卓瑪舒太太本底 leh kā 阮爸母 tàu 摒掃，有四个 gín-á，厝裡眞欠跤手，所以我 khah 大漢以後，就 tàu 照顧 in ê gín-á，無疑悟 tī 我八歲 ê 時，卓先生 suah 來過身去，卓老太太就 kā 卓瑪舒太太 kah hit 四个 gín-á 接去 tuà，put-jî-kò 伊 buaih tih 我。」

瑪俐問講：「落尾 leh？」

「落尾夏檬（Hammond）太太看我眞 gâu 顧 gín-á，就收留我。伊有八个 gín-á，其中六个是雙生 á。後--來 in 翁過身，伊 kah gín-á lóng 搬 tsáu 去，所以我 tiòh-ài 去孤兒院 ah。雖然 hia 已經人 kheh 人，in 姑不將 mā tiòh 收我。」

瑪俐問：「Hit kuá 太太對你好 bô？」

Tsit 時陣安妮 ê 面 suah 規个紅起來，講 tiòh 歹勢歹勢：「啊……in honnh……有想 beh 對我好啦，只不過 in 有 siunn tsē 代誌 ài 操煩，而且 in lóng tsiok sàn-tsiàh，卓瑪舒太太 in 翁 koh 定定 lim 酒醉。」

聽到 tsia，瑪俐無 koh 問落去 ah，伊心肝內 tsiok m̄ 甘 ê，安妮有影眞可憐，莫怪會 hiah-nī 向望有一个眞正 ê 家。伊若 hōo 安妮 kah in 做伙 tuà kám 好？馬修自底就想 beh án-ne 做，而且安妮應該是一个善良 koh 乖巧 ê gín-á。

第四章
重要 ê 決定

　　瑪俐 kah 安妮來到史平雪太太 ê 厝，史太太看 tiòh in ê 時有小 khuá-á 驚一 tiô，伊講：「我無想 tiòh 今 á 日會看 tiòh 恁 neh ！安妮，你好 bô ？」

　　安妮細聲 ìn：「我眞好，多謝你。」

　　瑪俐講：「阮 tú-tiòh 一个問題。阮進前是 kā 羅伯（Robert）講 beh ài 一个查埔 gín-á，是 án-tsuánn 伊 suah 安排查某 gín-á hōo 阮？」

　　史太太講：「啥物！伊 ê 查某 kiánn kā 我講恁 beh tih 查某 ê neh ！」

瑪俐講：「孤兒院發生 tsit 款錯誤，kám ē-tàng kā 伊 tshuā tò 轉去？」

史太太講：「應該 ē-tàng，m̄-koh 武維桃（Blewett）太太進前講伊需要一个查某 gín-á kā 伊 tàu 跤手，伊有真 tsē gín-á，安妮 ē-tàng kā 伊 tàu 顧。」

瑪俐自來 to m̄-bat 見過武太太，put-jî-kò tàk-ke lóng 知影伊 tsit 个人惡 koh tàng-sng，幾若个 íng 過 bat kā 伊 tàu 跤手 ê 查某 gín-á lóng 講 in kiánn mā tsiânn gâu tsau-that 人。想 tiȯh tsia--ê，瑪俐 suah liȯh-á 躊躇 kám beh kā 安妮交 hōo tsit 款人家。

史太太講：「Tú 好武太太 liâm-mi mā beh 來 tshuē 我，咱就順 suà 來 kā tsit 件代誌處理 hōo 好。」

史太太請瑪俐 kah 武太太來客廳坐，交代安妮去坐 tiàm 邊 á ê 椅頭 á。

看 tiȯh 歹面腔 ê 武太太，安妮雙手出力 lȧk 做伙，心肝內想講：「我 kám 真正 ài kah tsit 个惡 khiȧk-khiȧk ê 阿 sáng tuà 做伙？」ná 想 ná 想，煩惱、驚惶 ê 目屎強 beh liàn 落來。

史太太先 kā 武太太說明孤兒院 ê 失誤，koh 講：「前幾工有聽你講 beh ài 一个查某 gín-á 來 tàu 跤手，tú 好伊 ē-tàng hōo 你。」

武太太 kā 安妮自頭看到尾，講：「我若是收留你，你 ài 乖乖 á 聽話，ài ē-hiáu 看人目色 mā tiòh ài 有禮貌，阮 tau m̄ 是 hōo 你白食白睏 ê，有聽 tiòh bô？」

武太太 kā 瑪俐講：「Án-ne 我就 kā 伊接收落來，你若無反對，我 beh tshuā 伊 tò 轉去 ah。」

瑪俐講：「M̄-koh，我 kah 阮阿兄應該 mā beh 領養安妮，我只是想 beh 了解是 án-tsuánn 會 tîng-tânn niā，我 tsit-má ài 趕緊 tshuā 伊 tò 轉去 ah。」講了，伊 kah 安妮就 peh tsiūnn 馬車離開。

Tī 馬車頂安妮問瑪俐：「你 tú-tsiah 講 beh hōo 我 tuà tī 靑瓦厝，kám 有影？抑是我 leh 眠夢？」

瑪俐講：「我建議你上好 ài 小 tsún-tsat 一下 á 你 ê 想像力，我 iáu 未完全確定。」

「你若 ē-tàng 收留我，你叫我做啥物 lóng 好。」安妮溫馴 á 講。

In 轉來到靑瓦厝了後，瑪俐 kā 馬修講發生 ê 代誌。

「準若是我 tsiok 佮意 ê 狗 á，我 mā 無 ài 送 hōo 武太太，koh khah 免講是安妮！」馬修講。

瑪俐 mā 承認伊 kah 武維桃太太 tsit 種人 bē hàh，就講：「而且你 kah 安妮若像眞有緣，所以我同意收留伊。」

隔轉工瑪俐 kā 安妮講肯 hōo 伊留落來做伙 tuà。

安妮講：「Án-ne，我應該 án-tsuánn 稱呼你？」

「叫我瑪俐就好。你若叫我高小姐，我 tian-tò bē 慣 sì。」瑪俐講。

「我若直接叫你瑪俐，tsiok bô 禮貌 neh！」

「你若是好禮 á 叫就 bē 啊！咱亞檬里 ê 人 lóng mā 叫我瑪俐。」

安妮 koh 問另外一个問題：「我 tī tsia kám ē-tàng 交 tioh 好朋友？我一直向望有一个好朋友。」

「白黛娜（Diana Berry）就 tuà tī 附近，伊 kah 你 pênn 歲，是一个真乖 ê gín-á，你若 tú-tioh 伊 ài khah 有禮貌 leh，in 阿母 m̄ 肯 hōo 伊 kah 無教養 ê 查某 gín-á tàu 陣。」

安妮聽了真歡喜，問講：「黛娜生做啥物款？希望伊 ê 頭毛 m̄ 是紅 ê，我有紅頭毛就已經 tsiok 害 ah，我無 ài 我 ê 好朋友 mā 是紅毛 ê。」

瑪俐講：「黛娜生做婿噹噹，伊 ê 頭毛烏 sìm-sìm、烏仁金 sih-sih、tshuì-phué 粉牙 á 粉牙，比婿 koh khah 要緊 ê 是，伊乖 koh 巧喔！」

安妮講：「好佳哉！因爲我知影我 ka-kī 無婿，所以我 ê 好朋友若是眞婿就上 kài 好 ah。」

Beh 睏進前，安妮想 tiòh 瑪俐吩咐伊 ài 祈禱，就坐 tiàm 窗 á 邊 ê 椅 á，先 nauh 講：「我 tsit-má beh 假做我 tsiok 婿、tsiok lò，穿一領有白色 lè-sir ê 禮服，烏頭毛頂 kuân koh 插一支金 siak-siak ê 眞珠 tsiam。」

想到 tsia，安妮 bē 顧得祈禱，隨衝去照鏡，suah kan-na 看 tiòh 鏡內面 ka-kī ê 目睭是青色 ê，滿面全雀斑--liáu-liáu。

「你無婿！你無婿！你只是 tuà tī 青瓦厝 ê bái 安妮。是講，青瓦厝 ê bái 安妮 iáu khah 贏無依無倚 ê 安妮，tiòh bô？」

第五章

去教會

瑪俐問安妮：「Tsia-ê 衫你有佮意 bô ？」

安妮 tsim-tsiok 看瑪俐做 ê 三領新洋裝，看了細聲講：「我 ē-tàng 想像我真佮意。」

瑪俐講：「我 m̄ 是 ài 你想像，我看會出來你無佮意 tsit 三領洋裝，是 án-tsuánn hiooh ？」

安妮 iu-guân 細聲 ìn 講：「Tsit 三領……honnh……m̄ 是講……kài……婧啦！」

瑪俐講:「婿?Tsit 三領雖然無 lè-sir,m̄-koh 端莊 koh 大 pān。咖啡色角格 á kah 藍色素面 tsit 兩領是 beh hōo 你穿去學校 ê,有烏色、白色角格 á ê 綢 á 布 tsit 領是做禮拜 kah 主日學 ê 時 beh 穿 ê。看你進前 ê 衫 lóng 破 kôo-kôo,tann 有新衫 thang 穿 ah,你 ài 保持衫 ê 清氣整齊,mā 應該 ài 真感激才 tiòh。」

安妮講:「我是 tsiânn 感謝你親手做新衫 hōo 我,只是我 mā 想 beh 其中有一領是手 ńg 膨膨 ê,tsit 款衫最近 kài 時 kiânn。」

瑪俐講:「我感覺膨 ńg ê 衫看起來 tsiok 奇怪 neh!我 khah 愛素素 á、大 pān 大 pān ê 衫。Tsit-má 你 kā 洋裝好禮 á 吊起來,坐落來認真讀明 á 載主日學 ê 功課。」

瑪俐講 suah 就落去樓跤,安妮 kā hit 三領洋裝 koh 看一 pái 了後,大大下吐一个大氣,nauh 講:「我本來是向望有一領膨 ńg ê 白色洋裝,m̄-koh 看 pān 勢我 tiòh-ài ka-kī 想像其中一領有 lè-sir koh 有三層膨 ńg ah。」。

隔轉工早起,瑪俐人無爽快,無法度 tshuā 安妮去主日學,就 kā 安妮講:「你 kah 藺太太做伙去,ài 乖乖 á 聽話,m̄-thang luān-sú 看別人,抑是一直 ngiàuh 來 ngiàuh 去。Tsit 一 khoo 銀 hōo 你 tsah 去奉獻。」

安妮出門了後，沿路 ná kiânn ná khioh 玫瑰花 hām 金鳳花，koh kā 花 pinn 做一个大花 khoo，khoo tī 伊新點點 m̄-koh 素 kah 無花無草 ê 帽á頂。

伊感覺有花來妝 thānn，規个人看起來 ke guā 嬌 leh！落尾伊看藺太太無 tī 厝，就 ka-kī 一个人去教會 ah。

安妮 uì 教會 tò 轉來 ê 路裡，帽á頂 ê 花已經 lian 去 ah，就 kā 花 khoo tàn 掉。

「主日學有好 sńg bô？」瑪俐問伊。

「我無佮意，主日學實在有夠無聊。」安妮回答。

「你哪會 án-ne 講？」瑪俐驚一 tiô。

「馬傳道（Bell）一開始講 ê 祈禱文 lò-lò 長，而且阮 hit 班 ê 查某 gín-á 穿 ê 衫 lóng 有膨 ńg，kan-na 我無 niā-niā。」

「你上主日學 ê 時本來就無應該想手 ńg ê 代誌，我希望你認真上課。」

「有啊！我回答 tsiok tsē 問題啊！主日學結束，羅小姐（Rogerson）koh tshuā 我去看你 tī 教堂內面 ê 坐位 leh。實在是馬傳道講太久，koh 牧師講 ê 太無聊，我 m̄ 才無認真聽。」

瑪俐心內一方面 mā 認同傳道 kah 牧師 ê 講道 tsiok 無聊，一方面又 koh 認為伊應該 ài 罵安妮 tī 教會無專心，只是 m̄ 知啥因 tuann，伊 suah 罵 bē 出 tshuì。

　　Hit 禮拜五，瑪俐去拜訪藺太太，藺太太 kā 瑪俐講安妮帽 á 頂有花 ê 代誌。

　　瑪俐轉來就問安妮：「藺太太 kā 我講你去教會 ê 時，帽 á 頂有玫瑰花 kah 金鳳花，án-ne tsiok 奇怪 neh！」

　　安妮回答：「M̄-koh 眞 tsē 查某 gín-á ê 衫頂 kuân lóng 有 kat 花啊！」

　　瑪俐起性地罵伊：「Mài ìn tshuì ìn 舌！藺太太講，ta̍k-ke lóng leh 講你帽 á 頂有花 tsiok 怪 ê，mā lóng 想做我 bē-hiáu 教 gín-á，竟然允准你 tsit 款妝扮去教會！」

　　安妮 ê 目屎 kiōng-kiōng beh 滴落來，講：「歹勢，我 m̄ 是刁工 ê，我 m̄ 知你會 siūnn 氣。我是看 tio̍h 眞 tsē 查某 gín-á ê 帽 á 頂 lóng 有插花，我 m̄ 才 tuè 人插。抑是你 kā 我送轉去孤兒院無要緊，雖然我會 tsiok 傷心，mā khah 贏你 hōo 人誤會。」

　　瑪俐講：「Mài 烏白講！我無 beh kā 你送轉去孤兒院，我只是 ài 你 kah 別个查某 gín-á kâng 款 niā。好啦！Mài koh 哭 ah，我有好消息 beh kā 你講，黛娜已經轉去 in tau ah，我 beh 去 kā in 阿母借紙樣，你 beh kah 我做伙去 bô？」

安妮隨 khiā 起來，雙手合掌細聲講：「我真煩惱 neh！伊若無佮意我 beh án-tsuánn？」

瑪俐講：「我知影黛娜一定會佮意你，put-jî-kò 你 ài 代先想辦法 hōo in 阿母佮意你。希望伊 iáu 未聽 tiòh 你帽á頂有花 ê 代誌，抑無，伊對你 ê 印象會無好。Koh 有，去到 in tau ê 時，你一定 ài tsiok 乖 koh tsiok 有禮貌，m̄-thang 講一 kuá 會驚 tó 人 ê 話。」

第六章
新朋友

　　安妮 kah 瑪俐做伙 kiânn 來到白家 ê 果坡農場，瑪俐 lòng 門，來開門 ê 是白太太，伊生做 thiau-lāng thiau-lāng，目睭仁是烏 ê，頭毛烏 sìm-sìm。

　　「來！請入來坐，所以 tsit 位小姑娘 á 就是恁 tú pun 來 iúnn ê？」

　　「無 m̄-tiȯh，伊是施安妮。」

　　白太太牽安妮 ê 手，問伊：「你好 bô？」

「多謝阿姆關心，我真好，只是心情有 tām-poh-á ak-tsak。」安妮講了隨 uat 頭細聲問瑪俐：「Án-ne 講應該 bē kā 伊驚 tioh 啦 honnh?!」

黛娜本來坐 tī 膨椅 leh 讀冊，看 tioh 瑪俐 kah 安妮就 kā 冊放落來，對 in 微微 á 笑。

「這是我 ê 查某 kiánn 黛娜。」「來！黛娜，你 tshuā 安妮去外口 ê 花園 tshit-thô，去看你 ê 花。」白太太講。

In 兩人出去 khiā tiàm 一欉大欉 ê 百合花邊 á，gāi-gioh gāi-gioh sio-tuì-siòng。

「啊！黛娜，你 kám 有可能佮意我，做我 ê 好朋友？」安妮先開 tshuì。

黛娜笑出來：「應該 ē-sái 啊！我真歡喜你來 tuà tī 青瓦厝，án-ne 就有人 kah 我做伙 tshit-thô ah。阮小妹 lóng siunn 細漢，我 kah in sńg 無路來。」

安妮講：「你 kám 願意 tsiù-tsuā，永遠做我 ê 好朋友？」

黛娜講：「好啊！咱 beh án-tsuánn tsiù-tsuā？」

安妮牽黛娜 ê 手：「咱手牽手，我先來。」

「我 tsit-má tī tsia tsiù-tsuā，海水會 ta，石頭會爛，我永遠會對我 ê 結拜姊妹 á 黛娜忠誠。好 ah，換你學我講，只要 kā 你 ê 名改做我 ê 名就好。」

黛娜 ná 笑 ná tsiù-tsuā，了後講：「安妮你人眞 sim-sik neh，我感覺我會眞佮意你。」

瑪俐 hām 安妮 beh 轉去 ê 時，黛娜一直送 in 到溪邊，koh kah 安妮 iok-sok 明 á e-poo beh 做伙 sńg。

安妮 kā 瑪俐講：「我 tsit-má 是全島上快樂 ê 查某 gín-á！阮明 á 載 beh 做伙起一間尪 á 厝，伊會借我一本冊 koh beh 教我唱歌，我 tsiok 希望 ē-tàng 送伊一項物件。你 kám 知影我 kuân 伊兩公分？伊比我 ke 眞膨皮，m̄-koh 伊講想 beh khah 瘦一點 á，我感覺伊會 án-ne 講是驚我嫌 ka-kī siunn 瘦。」

瑪俐講：「我是 khah 煩惱你 siunn 厚話，一支 tshuì gâu thih-siông，害黛娜 ê 耳 á 歹去。你 ài 會記得，m̄ 是規工 lóng leh tshit-thô niā-niā，厝內 ê 工課 mā tiȯh-ài 做 neh！」

轉去到厝，馬修講有一个禮物 beh 送安妮，就 uì 褲袋 á jîm 一跤袋 á 出來，「聽講你愛食 tsioo-kóo-lè-tòo，來！我有買一 kuá-á beh hōo 你食。」

瑪俐講：「Aih-ioh！食 tse 對腹肚 kah tshuì 齒 lóng 無好 neh！」瑪俐看 tiȯh 安妮 leh bih-tshuì，隨

講：「好啦！Mài koh beh 哭 beh nih ah，既然馬修已經買 ah，你當然 ē-tàng 食，m̄-thang 做一 khùn 食了了喔！」

安妮講：「Bē 啦！我 e 暗先食一塊，tshun ê 我 kám ē-tàng 一半送 hōo 黛娜？我若 pun 伊一半，糖 á 食 tio̍h 會 ke 眞甜，我 tsiok 歡喜有物件 thang kah 伊公 ke 食。」

暗時安妮去睏了後，瑪俐 kā 馬修講：「Tsit 个 gín-á tsiah-nī pun-tiunn，實在無簡單。雖然才來三禮拜 niā-niā，就若親像已經來 tsiok 久 ah。好啦！我承認我當初 mā 想 bē 到會愈來愈佮意伊。你 mài kā 我講你早就知 ah 喔！」

第七章
去學校讀冊

　　九月份開始安妮就去學校讀冊，亞檬里學校是一棟白色 ê 建築物，內面有一間大教室，教室 ê 書桌 á lóng 是 uì 頂 kuân 掀開 ê。

　　安妮 tī 學校 tò 轉來 ê 時，kā 瑪俐講：「我感覺我會眞佮意去讀冊，因爲有義茹比（Ruby Gillis）hām 布知利（Tillie Boulter）tsit kuá 朋友，m̄-koh 黛娜 iáu 是我上好 ê 朋友。Koh 有安琵詩（Prissy Andrews）kah 義莎拉（Sara Gillis）講我 ê 鼻 á tsiok 媠，這是頭一 pái 有人 o-ló 我 ê 外表，伊講 ê kám 是眞 ê？我 ê 鼻 á kám 有影媠？」

瑪俐 ìn 講：「Bē-bái 啊！」其實伊感覺安妮 ê 鼻 á 確實真好看。

　　三禮拜後，安妮 kah 黛娜做伙 kiânn 路去學校 ê 時，黛娜講：「萊義柏（Gilbert Blythe）今 á 日會來學校 ah，伊規个歇熱 lóng 去 tuà tī 親 tsiânn hia。進前有一段時間 kah in 阿爸去西部發展，lóng 無來學校讀冊，所以現此時雖然是讀六年 ê，事實上已經十四歲 ah。」

　　In 兩人 kiânn 入去教室，坐 tiàm 兩塊排做伙 ê 書桌 á hia。

　　黛娜細聲 kā 安妮講：「坐 tī 你對面 hit 个人就是萊義柏，你看伊有緣投 bô？」

　　安妮 kā 萊義柏影一下，看 tiȯh 伊生做 lò-lò，咖啡色 ê 頭毛 khiû-khiû。Kâng tsit 時陣萊義柏 mā tshuì 笑目笑 leh 看安妮，尾 á koh kā 安妮 sái 目尾。

　　安妮 mā 細聲 kā 黛娜講：「伊有影生做 tsiok 緣投啦！M̄-koh siunn 過頭大膽，竟然 kā 生份人 sái 目尾，實在真無禮貌。」

　　其實，e-poo 發生 ê 才是大代誌。

　　菲利布（Philips）老師 tī 教室後壁教安琵詩一條數學 ê 時，其他 ê 學生無半个 leh 認真學，有 ê leh 食蘋果，有 ê leh 畫圖，有 ê tshi-bú-tshih-tshū leh 講話。

萊義柏想 beh siânn 安妮注意伊，但是安妮一直看窗 á 外，gōng 神 gōng 神 leh 做伊 ê 美夢。

萊義柏 iáu m̄-bat tú-tiòh 查某 gín-á buaih tshap 伊 ê，就刁工 giú 安妮長長 ê 兩條油 tsiàh 粿，koh tī 安妮 ê 耳 khang 邊講：「紅菜頭！紅菜頭！」

安妮 uàt 頭 kā 伊 gîn，koh khiā 起來嚷：「你真好大膽！」Suà 來就 kā 伊 ê 細塊寫字枋 giâ kuân-kuân，大大力對萊義柏 ê 頭殼頂 kā hám 落去，hám 一下寫字枋 suah liòh-á pit 開。

老師隨衝過來，「施安妮同學，你是 leh 創啥物？」

安妮無 ìn 話，伊才 buaih 承認 tú-tsiah 有人叫伊紅菜頭。

「是我 m̄-tiòh，我 tú-tsiah kā 伊創 tī。」萊義柏解 sueh。

老師完全 m̄ 聽萊義柏 ê 解 sueh，講：「我教出來 ê 學生竟然性地 tsiah-nī bái！安妮，去烏枋頭前罰 khiā！」

安妮無哭 mā 無頭 lê-lê，因為伊 iáu leh 風火頭。

放學 ê 時陣，安妮頭 giàh kuân-kuân，大 huàh 大 huàh 一直向前 kiânn，萊義柏 tuè tī 後壁，ná jiok

ná 講：「安妮！我 tú-tsiah 無應該笑你，我 kā 你會失禮，請你 mài siūnn 氣。」

安妮做伊繼續 kiânn，iu-guân m̄ tshap 伊。

黛娜 kah 安妮做伙 kiânn 轉去 ê 時，黛娜講：「安妮，你 mài án-ne 啦！」

安妮講：「我永遠 bē 原諒萊義柏。」

黛娜講：「萊義柏就是愛創 tī 人，學校所有 ê 查某 gín-á lóng bat hōo 伊 tih 過！伊進前笑我 ê 頭毛烏，koh 叫我烏鴉！」

「Hōo 人叫紅茱頭是上食力 ê，伊 siunn 超過，已經嚴重傷害 tiòh 我 ê 心 ah！」

尾手有 koh khah 精彩 ê 發展。

第八章
萊義柏

菲利布老師講:「最近 tàk-ke 中晝頓 lóng 食 kah siunn uànn tò 轉來上課,uì 今 á 日開始,恁 lóng ài tī 我入來教室進前就轉來。」

中晝下課 ê 時間,tàk-ke lóng tsáu 去馬家 ê 雲杉園,安妮 tī 園內上遠 ê 所在 ná 散步 ná 輕聲 á 唱歌。

一時間,俄子彌(Jimmy Glover)大聲 huah:「老師轉來 ah!」

其他 ê 查某 gín-á tī 老師 kiânn 入來進前就轉去教室坐好勢 ah，m̄-koh hit-kuá tiȯh uì 樹 á 頂落來 ê 查埔 gín-á 就 khah 慢，安妮 mā hē 性命 tsáu 轉來，落尾是 hām hit 陣查埔 gín-á 同齊 tsông 到教室門口，in 入去到教室 ê 時，老師 tú 好 kā 伊 ê 帽 á 掛好。

安妮趕緊坐 hōo 好，規个人 phēnn-phēnn 喘。

菲利布老師無想 beh 一下手處罰十二个學生，總--是 mā tiȯh liȧh 一个來 thâi 雞 kà 猴。

「施安妮，你若 tsiah-nī 愛 kah 查埔 gín-á 做伙，我就 hōo 你機會，你 tsit-má 去坐 tiàm 萊義柏 ê 邊 á。」

其他 ê 查埔 gín-á lóng leh 偷笑，黛娜 ê 面色白死殺，安妮目睭 liȧh 老師金金看。

「我講 ê 你有聽 tiȯh bô？」老師問。

「有聽 tiȯh，我 liȧh 做你是 leh 講 sńg 笑。」安妮慢慢 á 講。

「我無 leh 講 sńg 笑。」老師面 á tshìn-tshìn。

一開始，安妮若像無 leh kā 老師信 táu，m̄-koh 後--來 iáu 是勉強 khiā 起來，kiânn 去對面，坐 tiàm 萊義柏 ê 邊 á，雙手 kā 面 om leh，phak tī 桌 á 頂。

別个 gín-á tshi-bú-tshih-tshū leh 講閒á話，笑kah kā-kā 叫 koh ngiáuh 來 ngiáuh 去，過一時á了後，才 tiām 靜落來，開始專心寫功課。

等無人 leh 看 ê 時，萊義柏 uì 伊 ê 屜á 提一塊粉紅á色、心形 ê 糖á出來，糖á頂 kuân 寫「你 tsiok 古錐 ê」。伊 kā 糖á輕輕á seh tī 安妮手 khiau kah 桌á ê giap-phāng。

安妮頭 giah 起來，kā hit 塊糖á ni leh tàn 落去塗跤，koh 大大力 kā 糖á tsàm kah 碎 kôo-kôo，了後繼續 phak 落去桌頂。

放學 ê 時，安妮轉去伊原來 ê 位，kā 所有 ê 冊、筆、墨，kah 數學課本 lóng 總提出來，khuán kah 眞整齊 khng tiàm hit 塊小 khuá-á 有 pit 痕 ê 寫字枋頂 kuân，koh kā 寫字枋 mooh leh。

「你是 án-tsuánn beh kā 所有 ê 物件 khuán 轉去？」黛娜 kah 安妮做伙 kiânn tī beh 轉去 ê 路裡問伊。

「我 buaih koh 去學校 ah。」

黛娜目睭 tènn 大大蕊，講：「瑪俐 kám 會允准你 tiàm 厝？」

「伊一定 ài 允准！我永遠 bē koh 轉去學校 ah！」

「Án-ne 我 beh án-tsuánn？老師一定會叫我去 kah hit 个顧人怨 ê 派果蒂（Gertie Pye）坐做伙，因爲伊 lóng ka-kī 一个人坐啊！我拜託你一定 ài 轉來學校上課。」

「你 beh ài 我做啥物 lóng ē-sái，獨獨 tsit-pái 我眞正無法度，mài koh 強迫我啦！」安妮講 kah 眞傷心。

「若 án-ne 後過眞 tsē 趣味 ê 代誌你 lóng bē-tàng kah 阮 tàu 陣做 neh！後禮拜 beh 拍球，你自來 iáu m̄-bat phah 過球，彼 tsiok 刺激 neh！Koh 有 beh 學新歌曲，koh 有 beh 去溪 á 墘朗讀新冊，你 m̄ 是上愛朗讀 ê？」

安妮已經決心無 ài 去學校 ah，伊轉去厝 kā 瑪俐講。

「烏白來！是 án-tsuánn buaih 去學校？」

「我無烏白來，你 m̄ 知影我今 á 日 tī 學校 hōo 人侮辱！」

「無論 án-tsuánn 你明 á 載 lóng ài 照常去學校上課！」

「Bē-tàng 啦，我絕對 buaih koh 轉去學校 ah，我會乖乖 tī 厝裡 ka-kī 讀冊學習，我絕對 bē koh 轉去學校 ah！」安妮 ná 搖頭 ná 講。

瑪俐決定先 mài kah 安妮講學校 ê 代誌，伊去 tshuē 藺太太 tsham-siông，看 beh án-tsuánn 處理 khah 好。

「若是我 honnh，我會 hōo 伊先暫時留 tī 厝裡，等伊氣 khah 消 ah，伊 ka-kī 就會想 beh koh 轉去上課。我建議你免 siunn tì 意。」

瑪俐就照藺太太 ê 意見，無 koh 再堅持安妮 ài 去學校，安妮 mā 眞正 ka-kī tī 厝裡學習讀冊、做家內事，等 e-poo 黛娜下課才 kah 伊 tshit-thô。

安妮 mā 已經 hē 決心，tsit 世人永遠 bē 原諒萊義柏。

第九章

茶會

「我 beh 去參加一个聚會，你 ē-tàng 邀請黛娜 e-poo 來咱 tau 泡茶食點心。」十月份一个拜六 ê 早起時 á 瑪俐 kā 安妮講。

「好，多謝你！我自早就想 beh tsio 伊來食茶 ah。」安妮聽 tiòh 真歡喜。

「你 mā ē-tàng 開咱 ka-kī sīnn ê 櫻桃醬來配餅 kah 雞卵糕。頂 pái 教會聚會了後 iáu tshun 半罐刺莓 á 汁，我 khǹg tī 客廳 ê 櫥 á 第二 tsàn，你 kah 黛娜若有興趣 mā thìng 好 thîn 一 kuá 去 lim。」

瑪俐出門了後，黛娜就到位 ah，伊穿一 su 洋裝來 lòng 門，若親像一个淑女。

安妮 mā 穿一 su 洋裝去開門。In 兩人假影是頭 pái 見面 án-ne leh 握手，黛娜 kā 帽 á 收好，兩个人就 tī 客廳坐落來。

「阿姆最近身體好 bô？」安妮學大人 ê 氣口講話。

「伊眞好啊！多謝你。高先生 e-poo kám 是 kā 馬鈴薯載去貨船 hia？」

「無 m̄-tio̍h，阮今年馬鈴薯收成眞好，希望恁阿爸 ê 收成 mā 眞好。」

「阮 ê 收成 kâng 款眞好，多謝你關心。講 tio̍h tse，今年你 kám 有 khioh-tio̍h tsiok tsē 蘋果？」

「有啊！Tsiok tsē neh！」安妮講到 tsia suah bē 記得 ài 假做大人，hiông-hiông 跳起來講：「咱來去外口 ê 果子園 khioh tshun ê 蘋果！」

In ná khioh 蘋果 ná 食，黛娜 tú 講 tio̍h 萊義柏 ê 時陣，安妮無想 beh 聽，就 tsio 黛娜入去厝內 lim 刺莓 á 汁。

伊 tshuē 一 poo 久才 tī 櫥 á ê 上頂 kuân tsàn 看 tio̍h 一罐有寫「刺莓 á 汁」ê kan-á，伊 kā kan-á kuānn 落來 kah 杯 á khǹg tī 一塊桶盤頂。

「來，免客氣喔！我 tú-tsiah 蘋果食 siunn tsē，已經飽 kah lim bē 落去 ah。」安妮講。

黛娜 ka-kī thîn 一大杯，tam 一 tshuì-á 講：「有夠好 lim ê！我以前哪 m̄ 知刺莓 á 汁 tsiah-nī 純？」

「你若佮意，就免客氣，ke lim 一 kuá。」

黛娜 thîn 第二杯，lim 了 koh suà 第三杯，講：「Tse 口味 kah 藺太太 ê 刺莓 á 汁完全無 kâng，tse ke tsiânn 純！」

「當然啊！瑪俐做 ê 一定 khah 好，伊是出名 ê gâu 煮食。伊有教我，m̄-koh 我真 hân-bān。有一 pái 我看 tiòh 梅 á 醬 ê 甕 á 內底有一隻淹死 ê niáu 鼠 á，我就 kā 死 niáu 鼠 hôo 起來，suah bē 記得問瑪俐 hit 甕梅 á 醬 beh án-tsuánn 處理，一直到伊 kā hit 甕 mooh 出來 ê 時，我才想 tiòh 死 niáu 鼠 ê 代誌，我大聲 huah：「M̄-thang lim！Hit 甕內底有死 niáu 鼠 á！阮 hit 陣 koh 有人客在場 neh！」「黛娜，你是 án-tsuánn？」

黛娜想 beh khiā 起來 suah khiā bē tsāi，手緊 mooh 頭殼 koh 坐落來。「我感覺……tsiok 艱苦……我想 beh……轉去 ah……」

「你 iáu-bē lim 茶 neh！我隨來泡。」

「我頭殼 tsiok gông，我想 beh 轉去 ah。」

安妮 kā 黛娜 ê 帽 á 提 hōo 伊戴，koh 陪伊 kiânn 到 in tau ê 圍牆 á 外，伊 ka-kī 才翻頭 tò 轉去，伊頭一 pái ê 茶會實在有夠失敗！

第十章
白太太 liảh 狂

隔轉工是禮拜，雨落規工，安妮無法度去 tshuē 黛娜 tshit-thô。拜一 e-poo 瑪俐叫伊去藺太太 in tau 提物件。

過無 guā 久，安妮 ná 哭 ná tsáu 轉來，伊 tsông 入來灶跤，規个人 phiann 去膨椅頂。

「是發生啥物大代誌？」瑪俐問伊。

安妮坐起來 háu 講：「藺太太今á日去白太太 in tau，白太太怪我頂禮拜六 hōo 黛娜 lim 酒 lim kah 醉茫茫，伊講我是無正經 ê 查某 gín-á，伊永遠 bē koh hōo in 查某 kiánn kah 我 tàu 陣 tshit-thô ah。」

　　瑪俐目睭 thí kah 大大蕊嚷講：「伊 lim 酒醉？你到底是 thîn 啥物 hōo 伊 lim？」

　　「Kan-na 刺莓 á 汁啊！我 m̄-bat 聽過 lim 彼會酒醉！」

　　「烏白來！」瑪俐 kiânn 去客廳 ê 櫥 á 頭前，看 tiȯh hit 罐寫「刺莓 á 汁」ê kan-á tī 上頂 kuân tsàn。

　　Hit 罐是瑪俐伊上 tsāi 手 ê 烏莓 á 酒，伊 mā 想 tiȯh hit 罐刺莓 á 汁是 khǹg tī 地下室，m̄ 是 khǹg tī 客廳 ê 櫥 á 內。

　　伊 tò 轉去灶跤，也好氣也好笑講：「你 tsiânn-sit 眞 gâu 惹代誌！你 hōo 伊 lim ê 是烏莓 á 酒，m̄ 是刺莓 á 汁，kám 講你分 bē 清？」

　　「我無 lim m̄ 知啊！我 beh án-tsuánn 才好？In 阿母認定我是刁故意 ê。」

　　「好啦，mài koh 哭 ah，你 m̄ 是刁工 ê，你 ē-tàng 去 kā 白太太講一切 lóng 是意外、誤會。」

　　「我感覺我無法度面對伊。」安妮吐一个大氣，「Kám ē-tàng 拜託你去 kā 伊講，伊有可能會聽你 ê。」

「好啊！我會 kā 伊講，你 m̄-thang koh háu，無要緊啦！」

事實上代誌無 hiah-nī 簡單，安妮看 tiȯh 瑪俐 tò 轉來 ê 面色就知 ah。

「伊 buaih 原諒我，是 bô？」安妮真傷心問瑪俐。

「真正是 honnh！白太太是我看過 ê 人 tang 中，上 kài 無理 ê。我已經 kā 伊講一切 lóng 是誤會，你 mā m̄ 是刁工 ê，無論我 án-tsuánn pué-huē，伊 lóng m̄ 聽！」瑪俐講 kah 氣 phut-phut，尾手就 kiânn 入去灶跤。

Hit 暗，安妮 háu kah 睏去，瑪俐輕聲入去伊 ê 房間看。

「可憐 ê gín-á。」瑪俐細聲講。伊輕輕 á kā 安妮 khàm-tiȯh 面 ê 一 tshok-á 頭毛 pué 開，koh ànn 落來輕輕 á tsim 伊 háu kah 紅 kòng-kòng ê tshuì-phué。

隔轉工透早，安妮 kuānn 伊 ê 冊 kah 寫字枋 uì 樓頂落來，伊講：「Tann 我已經永遠失去換帖 ê，我 kan-na tshun 一條路……就是轉去學校讀冊 ah。」

瑪俐雖然驚一 tiô，總--是伊 mā 真歡喜安妮總算 beh koh 轉去學校讀冊。

　　班上 ê 查某同學 lóng 眞 siàu 念伊，koh khah 歡迎伊 tò 轉來。李茹美（Ruby Gillis）hōo 伊三粒梅á糖，馬拉咪（Ella May McPherson）送伊一蕊紙áu ê花，波佳蒂（Katie Boutler）送伊一支空 kan-á thang té phang 水。

其實 mā m̄ 是 kan-na in 歡喜安妮 tò 轉來 niā。中晝食飽，有一粒大蘋果 khǹg tī 伊 ê 桌 á 頂，伊大 tshuì 開開 tng beh 咬落去 ê 時，才 hiông-hiông 想 tiòh tsit 款蘋果 kan-na 萊家果子園有種，一定是冤仇人萊義柏 khǹg ê！

伊隨 kā 蘋果 tàn 落去塗跤，bē-su 有毒 leh，koh 緊用手巾 á kā 手 tshit-tshit leh。

無論如何，安妮 mā 是眞歡喜 ē-tàng tò 轉去學校 kah 朋友做伙，伊 tsit-má ài 坐 tiàm 安咪妮（Minnie Andrews）邊 á，m̄-koh 伊 tsiok 思念黛娜。

「黛娜今 á 日若像有 leh 對我笑。」伊 kā 瑪俐講。

第二工早起，安妮收 tiòh 一張字紙 kah 一个包裹，內面寫：

我上親愛 ê 安妮：

阮阿母 m̄ 准我 tī 學校 kah 你講話抑是 tshit-thô，m̄ 是我無 ài kah 你 tàu 陣，請你 mài siūnn 氣。我 tsiok 思念你 ê，我 mā 無佮意派果蒂。我用最近上 kài 時 kiânn ê 紅色衛生紙做一張 tsu-giap hōo 你，咱全校 kan-na 三个查某 gín-á 知影 án-tsuánn 做喔！希望你若看 tiòh 就會想起我 iu-guân 是你 ê 換帖 ê。

白黛娜親筆

安妮回批 hōo 伊：

我上親愛 ê 黛娜：

你 ài 聽恁阿母 ê 話，我當然 bē siūnn 氣。你送我 ê 禮物我會永遠好好 á 寶惜，安咪妮人是真好，只是 khah 無想像力 niā。我已經有你 tsiah-nī 好 ê 好朋友 ah，我無需要其他 ê 朋友。

你規世人 ê 好朋友施安妮（mā 是柯蒂莉）親筆

註：E 昏暗 leh 睏 ê 時，我會 kā 你 ê 批 khǹg tiàm 枕頭跤。

第十一章
佳哉有安妮

　　安妮決心 beh 認眞 phah-piànn 讀冊提頭名，萊義柏 mā 有 kâng 款 ê phah 算。

　　In 兩个人開始競爭，每一科 lóng 想 beh 考第一，所以通常若 m̄ 是安妮第一就是萊義柏頭名。

　　學期結束了後，in lóng 升 khí-lí 國中，mā 開始學新 ê 科目，其中數學 tsit 科對安妮來講，上 kài 困難 ê 就是幾何學。

　　安妮 kā 瑪俐 sèh-sèh 唸講：「啊！這眞正 tsiok 煩 ê，

菲利布老師講我對幾何學 sa 無 tsáng，m̄-koh 萊義……我是講別人 lóng 真 gâu，連黛娜 to 真厲害，啊……我 tsiok 想伊 ê。」

正月有一暗 tng leh 落雪，安妮 tī 灶跤食飯桌讀冊，馬修坐 tī 膨椅 tuh-ku，瑪俐去謝禮鎮（Charlottetown）聽加拿大總理演講。

安妮 tsiok 想 beh 停落來看小說，又 koh 驚伊若無繼續練習數學，明á載幾何學考試會輸 hōo 萊義柏。

Hiông-hiông 外口積雪 ê 路裡，有 tsáu 倚來 ê 跤步聲，然後黛娜大力 kā 門開--開衝入來。

「發生啥物代誌？ Kám 是恁阿母原諒我 ah？」安妮驚一 tiô 問伊。

黛娜講：「你緊來！阮小妹破病 kah tsiok 嚴重 ê，應該是去 tì-tio̍h háu 喘（croup），阮爸母 lóng 去謝禮鎮 ah，in 出門進前有請瑪椒（Mary Joe）來照顧阮，m̄-koh 伊 bē-hiáu 處理 háu 喘 ê 病人，我煩惱 kah！」

馬修無講無 tànn 就 khiā 起來提伊 ê hiû-á kah 帽á，kiânn 出去外口。

安妮 ná 穿 hiû-á ná 講：「無要緊，馬修已經去請醫生 ah！」

黛娜哭講：「Huān 勢所有 ê 醫生 lóng 去謝禮鎮聽演講 ah！」

「免煩惱，你 mài 哭，你 bē 記得我以前照顧過哈樣太太 ê 三對雙生 á！In 以早定定 tì-tiòh háu 喘，我知影 ài án-tsuánn 處理啦！恁 tau 可能無 háu 喘藥 á，我先來去 khèh 一 kuá。」

In 兩个人做伙 kiânn tī kian 霜 ê 路裡，趕去黛娜 in tau。

三歲 ê 咪咪（Minnie May）有發燒，伊 háu 喘 ê 喘氣聲規間厝 lóng 聽會 tiòh。

「咱代先 ài hiânn tsiok tsē 燒水，來！茶 kóo 我已經 té tīnn ah，瑪椒你 ke 添 kuá 柴去爐 á 內，其實你應該早就 ài 想 tiòh，àh-tiòh ài 我提醒！」

安妮 kā 咪咪飼藥 á 了，就騙 hōo 伊睏。

安妮 kah 黛娜規暝 lóng 坐 tiàm 咪咪 ê 眠床邊陪伊，藥罐 á 內 ê 藥 á 食 kah 一滴 to 無 tshun。

馬修去到 tsiok 遠 ê 四平沙（Spencervale） 才 tshuē 有醫生，到 kah 半暝三點 in 來到位 ê 時，咪咪已經 khah 快活睏去 ah。Thiám kah 虛 leh-leh ê 安妮，mā 才放心 hām 馬修 tò 轉去。

安妮一直睏到 e-poo 才起床，伊衫á 褲穿好落來樓跤，看 tiȯh 瑪俐已經轉來 tī 灶跤 tshiah 膨紗。

瑪俐講：「你一定腹肚 iau ah，中畫飯 tī 烘爐頂，櫥á 內有梅á 醬 thang 配。馬修有 kā 我講昨昏 ê 代誌 ah，你先食飽才 koh 講。」

等安妮食飽，瑪俐講：「Tú-tsiah 白太太有來，伊一直講 beh kā 你 sueh 多謝，我堅持 ài hōo 你睏，所以無 kā 你叫。伊講 in 細漢查某 kiánn ê 命是你救轉來ê，醫生 mā án-ne 講。白太太 tsiânn 後悔進前因為烏梅á 酒 ê 代誌 m̄ 原諒你，伊 tsit-má 知影你真正 m̄ 是ㄅ工 ê ah，伊希望你 ē-tàng 原諒伊，mā 繼續 kah 黛娜 tàu 陣。」

安妮歡頭喜面問講：「我 tsit 陣 kám ē-tàng 去 in tau？我轉來會 kā 碗箸洗清氣。」

「好，緊去緊去，用 tsáu ê khah 緊！」瑪俐 tsiah 講 suah，安妮 bē-hù 穿 hiû-á 就 tsông 出去 ah。

第十二章
第一 pái 過暝

二月份一工暗暝，安妮 kā 瑪俐講：「明 á 載是黛娜 ê 生日，in 阿母講我 ē-tàng 去 in tau 睏 tī 客房過暝 neh！阮會代先去學校 ê 音樂會，拜託你一定 ài 允准我去，kám 好？」

瑪俐一開始無同意 hōo 安妮去別人 tau 過暝，落尾是因為馬修堅持才勉強來答應安妮。

第二工暗時，安妮 kah 黛娜 tuè 黛娜 ê 表兄弟做伙坐雪車去參加音樂會。

所有 ê 表演安妮 lóng 眞佮意，獨獨萊義柏 leh 朗讀伊 ka-kī 寫 ê 詩 hit tang 陣，安妮無愛聽，就刁工提冊出來看。

　　In 轉去到厝 ê 時已經 tsiok uànn，厝裡所有 ê 人 lóng leh 睏 ah，in 兩人就 nih 跤尾入去客房外口 ê 客廳。黛娜講：「Tsia tsiok 溫暖 ê，咱就 tī tsia 換衫。」

　　In 睏衫換好，安妮提議講：「咱來比賽看啥人 tsáu khah 緊！」

　　In 衝過客廳 kah 客房 ê 門，同齊跳 khí-lí 眠床頂。無疑悟棉被下跤 suah 有物件 leh tín 動，koh 哀一聲講：「阿彌陀佛喔！」

　　In 兩个驚一下趕緊 tsông 出房間，peh 去樓梯頂。「彼是啥物碗糕？」安妮細聲問。

　　黛娜笑講：「彼是大姑婆曹淑芬（Aunt Josephine），伊是阮阿爸 ê 大姑，tuà tī 謝禮鎭，已經七十歲 ah，人眞古派。咱姑不將 tiòh-ài 去 kah 咪咪睏 ah，只是伊 leh 睏 tsiok gâu kā 人踢！」

　　大姑婆第二工無來食早頓，安妮早頓食飽就趕緊 tò 轉去，e-poo 伊 koh 去 tshuē 藺太太處理一 kuá 雜事。

　　「聽講你 kah 黛娜昨暗 kā 可憐 ê 大姑婆驚一下半小死，黛娜 ê 阿母 kā 我講大姑婆性地眞 bái，伊氣 kah m̄ kah 黛娜講話 ah。」藺太太講。

「這 bē-tàng 怪黛娜，lóng 是我 m̄-tiòh，是我講 beh 比賽看啥人 khah 緊跳 khí-lí 眠床頂 ê。」

「我 to 知影一定是你 leh pìnn 鬼 pìnn 怪！Tsit-má 惹麻煩 ah。大姑婆本來 beh 來 tuà 一個月，tann 伊 suah 氣一下講明 á 載就 beh tsáu ah。Koh khah 食力 ê 是，伊本來答應 beh tàu 出錢 hōo 黛娜去上 ê 音樂課 mā 反悔 ah，所以黛娜 ê 爸母 tsit-má 頭殼 mooh leh 燒，因爲大姑婆 put-tsí-á 好 giàh，in 想 beh kah 伊保持好 ê 關係。」

安妮聽了隨 tsông 去黛娜 in tau，tī 灶跤門口 tú-tiòh 黛娜。

「聽講大姑婆氣 kah buaih tuà tsia，你哪會無 kā 伊講 lóng 是我害 ê？」

「我絕對無可能做 tsit 款代誌，我 m̄ 是 jiàu-pê-á，何況我 mā 有 m̄-tiòh 啊！」

「我 tsit-má 就親身去 kā 大姑婆會失禮。」安妮講 suah 就 kiânn 去 lòng 客廳 ê 門。

「入來！」tsiok 歹 ê 聲嗽。

安妮 kiânn 入去，大姑婆坐 tī 火爐邊 leh tshiah

膨紗，伊掛一支金框 ê 目鏡，看起來惡 khiàk-khiàk。

「你是啥人？」

「我是 tuà tī 青瓦厝 ê 安妮，今 á 日我來 tsia beh kā 你會失禮。」

「是 án-tsuánn beh 會失禮？」大姑婆大聲嚷。

「因為跳去眠床頂 kā 你 heh 驚 tiòh ê 代誌 lóng 是我 m̄-tiòh，是我提議 beh 跳 ê，所以請你千萬 m̄-thang 怪黛娜。」

「Bē-tàng 怪伊 hiooh？ Kám 講伊無跳 khí-lí 眠床頂 nih？」

「因為阮只是感覺 án-ne sńg 真趣味 niā-niā，請你一定 ài 原諒阮。無論 án-tsuánn，你一定 ài 原諒黛娜，繼續贊助伊上音樂課，你若一定 beh siūnn 氣，請你氣我就好。」

大姑婆無 koh gîn-ònn-ònn，伊講：「今 á 日若換做是你，本來暗時睏 kah 好勢好勢，突然間有人跳 tsiūnn 你 ê 身軀頂，kā 你 heh 驚 tiòh，你 kám bē siūnn 氣？」

安妮回：「是有影真恐怖，但是請你體諒阮。因為阮 m̄ 知影有人睏 tī 眠床頂，m̄ 才會 kā 你 heh 驚 tiòh，

koh 再講，昨暗本來是阿姆答應 beh hōo 阮睏 tiàm 客房 ê。大姑婆你應該定定、mā 真慣 sì 睏客房 ah，m̄-koh 你若像我是孤兒，一定真歡喜頭 pái beh 睏客房 neh！」

大姑婆聽了笑哈哈講：「我 ê 想像力已經真久無用 ah，可能會小 khuá khê-khê！來，坐落來 kā 我講你 ê 故事。」

安妮講：「真歹勢，我 ài 先 tò 轉去 ah。希望你 ē-tàng 原諒黛娜，mā 希望你留落來，繼續 tuà tsia。」

大姑婆微微 á 笑：「你若 ē-tàng 來 tsia kah 我開講，我可能會繼續留 tī tsia。」

Hit 暗，大姑婆 kā 黛娜 ê 爸母講伊行李內底 ê 物件 lóng 總 beh koh 搬出來 khǹg 轉去客房。

「我已經決定 beh 留落來 tuà，我 mā 想 beh koh khah sik-sāi hit 个安妮，伊人 tsiok sim-sik，kā 我 lāng kah 笑 hai-hai。」

大姑婆後--來 tī hiah tuà 超過一個月，伊 beh 離開 ê 時 kā 安妮講：「你 ài 會記得 neh！你若有來謝禮鎮，一定 ài 來 tshuē 我，我會 hōo 你 tuà 上高級 ê 客房。」

第十三章
安妮 hōo 人刺激 tio̍h

Hit 冬 ê 八月，黛娜邀請 in 班 ê 查某 gín-á 去 in tau tshit-thô，in 決定 beh sńg 一个比賽叫做：「你 kám 有才調？」

派椒思（Josie Pye）代先講：「洪茉安（Jane Andrews），你 kám 有才調用一肢跤跳花園一 liàn，lóng 無停落來？」

洪茉安輸 ah，因爲伊一肢跤 kan-na 有才調跳半 liàn niā-niā。

Suà 來換安妮問派椒思 kám 有才調 kiânn tī 籬笆頂 kuân ？派椒思輕輕鬆鬆一下 á 就 kiânn 了 ah。

　　安妮講：「Kiânn 一塊 á 籬笆 niā 無啥物 thang 好臭屁 ê，我 sik-sāi 一个查某 gín-á，伊有法度 kiânn tī 厝頂。」

　　派椒思罵講：「我才 m̄ 相信！無可能有人有才調 tī 厝頂 kiânn，你 mā 無法度！」

　　「我一定有法度！」安妮大聲講。

　　「若 án-ne 你 kám 有才調 uì tsia peh-khí-lí 白家灶跤 ê 厝頂 kiânn ？」

　　雖然安妮驚 kah 規个面青 sún-sún，伊 iáu 是 kiânn 去灶跤外口 ê 樓梯跤，別个查某 gín-á lóng tuè tī 安妮後壁，in 無相信伊眞正 beh án-ne 做。黛娜講：「你 m̄-thang 啦！若 puȧh 落來會摔死 neh ！」

　　「我一定 ài 去，因爲這 iú 關我 ê 名聲，黛娜，萬一我若死去，我 ê 眞珠耳鉤就送你。」安妮交代。

　　安妮 peh 樓梯 ê 時 lóng 無人敢出聲，伊 peh 起到厝頂了後先 khiā hōo tsāi 才開始 kiânn，五、六步了後，伊 hiông-hiông 開始 bē 穩，手 tī 半空中畫一兩 liàn，就規个人 tsai 落來，伊先 uì 另外一 pîng 厝頂 tshu 落才 koh puȧh 落來塗跤。

黛娜 kah hia-ê 查某 gín-á lóng tsông 去伊 puȧh 落來 ê 所在，黛娜吱吱叫講：「安妮，你 kám 死去 ah？你哪會 lóng bē 講話 ah？」

頭殼 gông-gông ê 安妮坐起來講：「黛娜，我 iáu 活 leh，m̄-koh 我 ê 身軀完全無感覺。」

「Tó 位？你身軀 tó 位無感覺？」有人開始 leh háu。

安妮 iáu-bē ìn，白太太就 tsáu 過來 ah，安妮想 beh khiā 起來，suah 哀一聲 koh un 落去。

「你有要緊 bô？你 tó 位 leh 疼？」白太太問。

「我 ê 跤目會疼，我無法度 kiânn 轉去，我一肢跤 mā 跳 bē 轉去到厝！」

瑪俐 tú 好 tī 果子園內底，hiông-hiông 去看 tiȯh 白先生抱安妮 uì 山坡 kiânn 倚來。

Tsit 時陣，伊才知影 ka-kī 有 guā 愛安妮，對伊來講，全世界無啥物比安妮 koh khah 重要，伊趕緊衝過去，phēnn-phēnn 喘講：「白先生，發生啥物代誌？」

安妮 giȧh 頭講：「瑪俐，你免煩惱，我 peh khí-lí 白家 ê 厝頂，suah 無 tiunn-tî puȧh 落來，可能是跤目去 uáinn tiȯh，好佳哉我 ê ām-kún 無摔斷去。」

　　瑪俐趕緊 tshuā in 來灶跤，講：「白先生，請你抱
伊入來 tsia，先 hōo 伊 the tiàm 膨椅頂。」「Ai-iō-uê
啊！伊人哪會昏昏去 ah ！」

　　馬修 uì 田園轉來了後，就隨去請醫生，醫生看了後
講安妮 ê 跤目摔斷去。

　　後來瑪俐 phâng 暗 tǹg
去安妮 ê 房間，伊跤目
khōng 石膏 tó tī 眠
床頂。

安妮細聲問講：「你 kám 有同情我？」

「這是你 ka-kī 做得來 ê。」瑪俐 ná 講 ná kā 百葉窗關起來 koh 去點油燈。

「Ḿ-koh 若有人刺激你，問你 kám 有才調 kiânn tī 厝頂 leh ？」安妮問伊。

「我會照常 khiā tī 塗跤，管待 in 講我無才調。你 honnh ！眞正是烏白來！」

安妮吐一个大氣講：「請你 mài siūnn 氣，我無親像你 tsiah-nī 老步定，我一定 ài 接受派椒思 ê 挑戰，因爲我若無做 hōo 看，伊會一世人 kā 我 liū tsit 件代誌。」

「Suà 落來 ê 六、七个禮拜我 lóng 無法度 kiânn 路，萊……我是講每一个同學學習 ê 進度 tiānn-tiȯh 會比我 khah 緊，m̄-koh 我一定會堅強。」

「好啦！我 bē siūnn 氣，你免煩惱，先食飯才講。」

過後 ê 七个禮拜，有眞 tsē 人來看伊，有朋友提花 kah 冊來送伊，koh 順 suà kā 伊講一 kuá 學校發生 ê 代誌。

「瑪俐，tȧk 个人 lóng 對我 tsiok 好，連派椒思 to 來看我，我看伊可能眞後悔講我無才調 kiânn tī 厝頂；黛娜 kā 我講阮換新老師 ah，叫做徐蒂思（Muriel

Stacey），伊有金色 ê 頭毛 kah 藍色 ê 目睭，伊 ê 手 ńg 是全亞檬里上 kài 膨 ê，每一个拜五 e-poo 伊 lóng 要求 ta̍k 个學生 ài 背詩抑是戲劇，koh 會 tshuā 學生去校外研究植物 kah 鳥 á，我已經 tòng-bē-tiâu ah，我苦 bē 得隨轉去上課，因為我知影我一定會真佮意 tsit 个老師！」

瑪俐笑笑 á 講：「有一件代誌我是非常確定啦，你 uì 厝頂 pua̍h 落來完全無礙 tio̍h 你 ê tshuì 舌！」

第十四章
快樂 ê 聖誕節

　　安妮十月份轉去學校上課，一個月後，亞檬里學校 ê 學生開始準備聖誕節音樂會，這是徐蒂思老師 ê 建議，安妮興 tshih-tshih，put-jî-kò 瑪俐有無 kâng ê 看法。

　　「我無贊成辦 tsit 款音樂會，這會 hōo 學生 gín-á 規工想 tsia-ê 有--ê 無--ê，suah 無認真讀冊。」

　　「這是做善事，阮 beh 募款來做校旗。」

　　「烏白講！你根本就是愛 sńg niā-niā。」

「辦音樂會 tsiânn-sit 眞趣味啊！黛娜 beh 唱歌、我 beh 參加兩齣戲 koh 會朗讀兩首詩，我知影你無親像我 tsiah-nī 佮意音樂會，kám 講你無向望我有眞好 ê 表現？」

「我 kan-na 向望你會 khah tiānn-tiȯh leh ！等 tsia-ê lok-kò-sok-kò ê 活動 lóng 結束，你 mā khah 穩定落來 ah，我 tian-tò 會 khah 歡喜。」

安妮吐一个大氣了，就去後壁園 á 馬修 leh phuà 柴 ê 所在 tshuē 伊。

安妮 kā 馬修講音樂會 ê 消息。「這一定會是眞讚 ê 音樂會，我 mā 知影你會好好 á 表演。」馬修 bûn-bûn-á 笑，安妮 mā 對伊微微 á 笑。好佳哉伊有來 tshuē 馬修，馬修是一个 tsiânn 溫暖 ê 人。

十二月生冷 ê 一工，馬修 uì 外口 kiânn 入來灶跤，坐落來 thǹg 鞋。

安妮 kah 幾个 á 朋友 leh 練習音樂會 ê 表演，in ná 講 ná 笑。馬修第一 pái 注意 tiȯh 安妮 ê 衫 kah hia-ê 查某 gín-á 精差眞 tsē，in lóng 穿 hiánn 色、婧噹噹 ê 洋裝，是 án-tsuánn 瑪俐 hōo 安妮穿 ê lóng 是暗色兼古板 ê 衫？「我 beh 送伊一領婧衫做聖誕禮物。」伊去請藺太太 tàu-sann-kāng。

「替你揀一領洋裝送安妮？無問題！我看淺咖啡色應該真 hȧh 伊穿。你若無反對，我 mā ē-tàng ka-kī tshia。」藺太太講。

「Án-ne 就拜託你 ah，koh 有 honnh…… 聽講 tsit-má 手 ńg honnh……kah 以前無 kâng 款？若 bē siunn 麻煩，手 ńg kám ē-tàng 做 khah 新型 ê？」

「你是講膨手 ńg nih？安啦！免煩惱，這交 hōo 我處理。Tsit 款洋裝 tng 時 kiânn neh！」

聖誕節透早，安妮 uì 樓頂 tsáu 落來講：「瑪俐，聖誕節快樂！馬修，聖誕節快樂！」

馬修 kā 洋裝提出來，安妮問：「彼……彼……是 beh hōo 我 ê hiooh？」

伊 kā 新洋裝提 kuân 看，材質摸 tiȯh 幼 mī-mī、滑軟 á 滑軟，ām 領有一 lìn lè-sir，koh 有膨膨 ê 手 ńg，伊目 khoo 紅 ah。

「彼是送你 ê 聖誕禮物……eh……你是 án-tsuánn leh 流目屎？Kám 講你無佮意？」

安妮 kā 洋裝 phuȧh tiàm 椅 á 頂，笑笑 á kā 馬修講：「哪會無佮意？我愛 kah！多謝你，tsit 領洋裝 tsiok 婎 ê，尤其是 tsit 款膨手 ńg。」

「好啦！來食早頓，我是認為你無欠洋裝啦！既然馬修已經 tshuân hōo 你 ah，你 tiòh-ài 好好 á 寶惜。藺太太 koh 有 kah 一條 kâng 色 ê 緞帶 beh hōo 你 pàk 頭鬃，kah 你 ê 洋裝真 tàu-tah。」

早頓食飽，安妮 kah 黛娜約 tī 橋跤見面。

「大姑婆有禮物 beh 送你。」黛娜交 hōo 伊一个 kheh-á。

安妮 kā kheh-á 開--開，內底有一張卡片 kah 一雙皮 tshián-thua-á，面頂有金 sih-sih ê 珠 á、khian-á，koh kat 一隻緞帶做 ê 蝶 á。

「啊！這真正是我 tsit 世人上讚 ê 聖誕節！」

Hit 暗舉辦聖誕音樂會，結束 ê 時天頂已經滿天星 ah，安妮 kah 黛娜做伙 kiânn 轉去。

「Tàk-ke lóng tsiok 佮意你朗讀 ê 部份，koh 有你演戲 ài tsáu 落台跤 ê 時，一蕊玫瑰花 uì 你 ê 頭殼頂 lak 落來，我看 tiòh 萊義柏 kā 花 khioh 來袋落去褲袋 á，有夠浪漫 neh！」

「哪有！我才 m̄ 管 hit 个人 leh 創啥，永遠 to m̄！」

第十五章

紅頭毛無--去

四月份一工 e-poo，瑪俐 tò 轉來 ê 時安妮無 tī 灶跤，伊就去安妮 ê 房間 beh 提一支蠟條，看 tiòh 安妮規个人 phak tī 眠床頂。

「Ai-iō-uê！你 tī tsia 睏規晡 nih？」

「Ṁ 是！」安妮 iu-guân phak leh，頭 giàp tī 兩粒枕頭中央，lóng 無 giàh 起來。

「你是人無爽快 hiooh？」

「Ṁ 是，請你緊 tsáu，mài 看我。」

「Tann 你是 án-tsuánn？你 koh 做啥物大代誌 ah？Tsit-má 隨起來 kā 我講！」

安妮坐起來細聲講：「你看我 ê 頭毛。」

瑪俐 giȧh 蠟條倚近一下看，伊驚一 tiô！「施安妮！你是 leh 創啥，是 án-tsuánn 頭毛會變青色？」

「我知影是青色……我本來想講 tshìn-tshái 色 to 比紅色 khah 婿，無疑悟青頭毛 koh khah 慘十倍！」

「是 án-tsuánn 你 ê 頭毛會變青色？」

「我去染頭毛。」

「染頭毛！施安妮！是 án-tsuánn 你會做 tsit 款 hi-hua ê 代誌？」

「我 mā tsiok 後悔。我 kā 一个 huah-lin-long ê 阿伯買 ê，伊講頭毛染了會烏 sìm-sìm、婿噹噹。我本來 liȧh 做我 ê 頭毛會變 khah 婿講……。」

「你落來灶跤，咱試看染色 kám 洗會掉。」

無論瑪俐 án-tsuánn kā 洗 to 洗 bē 掉，安妮就堅持 buaih 出門，mā m̄ 肯去學校。

安妮 tȧk 工洗頭，一禮拜過 iáu 是洗 bē 掉。

「我看這真正無法度 ah，我 ài kā 你 ê 頭毛 ka 掉，

你 bē-tàng 一直留 tī 厝裡無去學校。」

瑪俐 kā 安妮 ê 頭毛 ka 短短。安妮去學校除了派椒思，無人 kā 笑。

「派椒思講我頭毛 án-ne 若親像稻草人，我本來 beh kā tủh，落尾就 suah-suah 去，原諒伊。」「你有要緊 bô？我 kám 是講話講 siunn 久害你頭殼疼？」看 tiỏh 瑪俐 leh 摸鬢邊，安妮問伊。

「我頭有 khah 好 ah，你繼續講無要緊，bē 礙 tiỏh 我，我已經慣 sì 慣 sì ah。」

其實瑪俐 án-ne 講就表示伊真愛聽。

第十六章
船 ê 事件

　　熱人有一工，安妮、黛娜、茹美 kah 茱安（Jane）去金爍湖湖邊 beh 演亞瑟王 ê 故事。In leh 討論啥人來演美麗 ê 少女伊蓮（Elaine），伊爲 tiòh 緣投 ê 蘭司羅公爵（Sir Lancelot）犧牲 ka-kī ê 性命。

　　安妮建議 ài 演 tsit 段眞浪漫 ê 劇情，「伊蓮過身了後，其他 ê 人 kā 伊 ê 死體 khǹg tī 船頂，然後 kā 船 sak 落去溪裡，船就 ûn-ûn-á 流去卡明拉城（Camelot）。黛娜，咱 ē-tàng 用恁阿爸 hit 隻舢舨 á 來準做故事內底 ê 平底船。」

「安妮，hōo 你演伊蓮，我 m̄ 敢 ka-kī 一个 tó tī 船頂流去溪 á。」黛娜講。

「無要緊，我來！」安妮講 suah 就踏入去船裡。「茹美，你演亞瑟王，茱安是語爾美皇后（Guinevere），黛娜你就是蘭司羅公爵。M̄-thang bē 記得，恁 lóng ài 去 tó 位 kah 我會合？無 m̄-tiȯh，tī 卡明拉城，啊……我是講 tī 水池 ê 對面 hit pîng。」

安妮 tó tī 船裡，雙手 sio-thȧh 貼 tī 胸坎，目睭 kheh-kheh，茱安講：「Kā 船 sak 落水。」

　　船 tú sak 落水 niā，就 tuè 水流出去 ah。安妮 tng leh 想像 ka-kī 是 tsiok 愛蘭司羅公爵 ê 伊蓮，一時間伊 suah 感覺舢舨 á 內底有水，就趕緊坐起來，看 tiȯh 船尾破一 khang put-tsí-á 大 khang，溪水直直 uì hit khang 灌入來，tann 船 teh-beh 沉落去 ah！

　　Tsit 隻船順水勢流向柴橋，lòng-tiȯh 老樹身做 ê 橋墩，安妮趕緊趁 tsit 个機會 peh-khì-lí 橋墩，kā 樹身 mooh leh，一跤踏 tī 樹身頂 phok 出來 ê 一 tsat-á 樹枝。才一目 nih，船就規个沉落去 ah。

　　Hia-ê 查某 gín-á 叫是安妮 tuè 船沉落去 ah，lóng 驚 kah 目睭 thí 大大蕊 leh siòng 水底，m̄-koh lóng 無看 tiȯh 安妮 ê 形影，尾手 in 一陣人就吱吱叫 tsông 入去樹林 á，無半个人注意 tiȯh 柴橋 hit pîng。

　　安妮聽 tiȯh in 規陣吱吱叫 ê 聲，mā 有看 tiȯh in 衝過去路邊。伊細聲講：「拜託趕緊 tshuē 人來救我！」

　　伊 m̄ 知影踏 tiàm hit tsat 樹枝有法度 tòng guā 久，每一秒 lóng bē-su 一世紀 hiah 久。安妮想講：「是 án-tsuánn iáu 無人來？」

　　Tng 當伊 teh-beh 溜落去 ê 時，有人 kò 船來 ah，原來是萊義柏。

　　伊 kò 來到橋跤，手伸向安妮，安妮本 tsiânn 實在 tsiok 無想 beh 牽萊義柏 ê 手，但是若無 án-ne 做，伊

liâm-mi 就 beh puàh 落去 ah！伊只好 kā 萊義柏 ê
手 giú-tiâu-tiâu，趕緊 peh-khí-lí 萊義柏 ê 船頂。

「是發生啥物代誌？」

「阮 leh 演伊蓮 hit 齣戲，我 tó tī 平底船……
eh……我 ê 意思是講 kò 船……過去卡明拉城，想 bē
到船 suah 開始入水，我 m̄ 才緊 mooh hit 支橋墩。
Kám ē-tàng 拜託你載我去岸邊？」安妮講話 ê 時 lóng
無看伊。

In 一下到岸邊，安妮就隨踏出去，面 á tshìn-tshìn
講：「眞多謝你。」Uàt 頭就 beh tsáu。

萊義柏 uì 船頂跳落來，giú 伊 ê 手 khiau 講：「安妮，咱 kám ē-tàng 做朋友？我 tsiânn-sit tsiok 後悔 hit 陣笑你 ê 頭毛，而且彼已經是真久以前 ê 代誌 ah，我感覺你 tsit-má ê 頭毛 tsiok 婿。」伊用熱誠 ê 眼神看安妮，害安妮 ê 心肝頭 phih-phȯk-tsháinn。

安妮翻頭 koh 想 tiȯh hit tang 陣萊義柏叫伊「紅菜頭」是 guá-ní-á 傷伊 ê 心，iáu 有，就是因為萊義柏，伊才會 tī 全班面頭前失面子，伊絕對 bē 原諒伊！

「無法度，萊義柏，我永遠 bē koh kah 你做朋友。」

「無要緊，施安妮，我 mā 永遠 bē koh 拜託你做我 ê 朋友 ah！」伊講了就跳轉去船頂。

萊義柏 kā 船 kò tsáu，安妮 ê 頭一直 giȧh kuân-kuân m̄ 看伊，其實安妮心內知知，伊 tsit pái 應該 ài 原諒萊義柏才 tiȯh。

Tī kiânn 轉去 ê 半路裡，安妮 tn̄g-tiȯh 黛娜 kah 茱安。黛娜驚一下講：「安妮！阮 lóng liȧh 做你沉落去 ah neh！你是 án-tsuánn 逃生 ê？」

安妮人 thiám kah，ìn 講：「我 mooh tī 柴橋 ê 一支橋墩，後--來萊義柏 tú-tshiāng 出現 kā 我救來岸邊。」

「喔，án-ne tsiok 浪漫 ê，所以後 pái 你 kám 會 kah 伊講話 ah？」

「當然 bē！」

後--來安妮 kā 瑪俐講：「我 buaih koh hiah-nī 浪漫 ah，我本 tsiânn 叫是 kā 頭毛染做烏色、想像 ka-kī 是伊蓮，tsia--ê lóng 是 tsiok 浪漫 ê 代誌，想 bē 到頭毛變做青色，koh 險險 á tū 死！我應該 ài khah 有智慧 leh，mài koh 惹事才 tiȯh。Uì tsit-má 開始，你會看 tiȯh 一个 khah 理性 ê 安妮。」

瑪俐 ìn：「若 ē-tàng án-ne 是上好啦！」

第十七章
大考

　　十一月份 ê 一工暗時，瑪俐 kā 安妮講：「老師今 á 日有來厝裡。」

　　安妮本來 tó tī 地毯 leh 看爐 á 內 ê 火，聽 tioh 瑪俐 ê 話，伊 giah 頭問講：「對老師真失禮 neh！我 hit 陣 tú 好出去。是 án-tsuánn 伊會來咱 tau？」

　　「伊來問我 kah 馬修 kám 有 beh hōo 你補習來準備皇后師範學院 ê 入學考試，你想 án-tsuánn？你 kám 有興趣去讀師範學院，後過做老師？」

「喔！我當然 tsiok 有興趣做老師啊！ M̄-koh án-ne 學費 kám bē ke 真貴？」

「學費 ê 代誌你免煩惱，我 kah 馬修已經決定 beh khiām 錢 hōo 你讀冊，阮一定 beh hōo 你受上好 ê 教育。」

安妮 kā 瑪俐 lám-tiâu-tiâu，講：「多謝你！我一定會認真 phah-piànn 讀冊來報答怎！」

Tsit 个特別 ê 班有安妮、萊義柏、茹美、茱安 kah 派椒思，in tak 工下課了後 lóng 留落來繼續準備入學考試。

安妮 kah 萊義柏之間 ê 競爭愈來愈激烈，而且下課以後 ê 時間，萊義柏會 kah 別个查某 gín-á 講笑，有時 á koh 會 kah in 做伙 kiânn 路 tò 轉去，m̄-koh 伊 kan-kan-á kah 安妮無 kau-tshap。

其實安妮並無想 beh án-ne 生。伊早就原諒萊義柏，bē siūnn 氣 ah，mā 想 beh kah 伊做朋友，只是這一切 lóng bē-hù ah。伊知影 beh 怪 tioh-ài 怪伊 ka-kī。

學期結束 hit 工，安妮 kā 所有 ê 課本搬去半樓 á，kā 瑪俐講：「我規學期已經 hē 性命 leh 讀冊，tsit-má 歇熱 ah，我 beh 認真來 sńg。」

九月份 ê 時，安妮 hioh 夠氣 ah，準備 beh 繼續 phah-piànn 讀冊。

Hit 多三月安妮滿十五歲，有一工瑪俐發現安妮已經比伊 khah lò ah。Hit 暗，馬修入去灶跤，竟然看 tioh 瑪俐 leh 流目屎，瑪俐罕得哭 neh！

「我是想 tioh 講安妮哪會大 tsiah-nī 緊！明年 kuânn 人伊可能去外地讀冊 ah，若 án-ne 我會 tsiok 想伊 ê。」

「伊 ē-tàng 定定 tò 轉來啊！」

瑪俐吐大氣講：「Mā 是 kah 伊一直 hām 咱 tuà 做伙無 kâng 啊！」

安妮真向望 thìng 好去師範學院讀冊，put-jî-kò 伊 ài 先通過考試。

六月份伊 kah 同窗做伙去謝禮鎮參加考試，hit 禮拜安妮 lóng tuà tī 大姑婆 hia。

「我感覺每一科 lóng 考 liáu bē-bái，kan-na 驚幾何 tsit 科 bē 通過。」安妮 kā 黛娜講。

「你一定會通過啦，免煩惱。」

事實上安妮 m̄ 是 kan-na 求通過 niā，伊想 beh 考比萊義柏 koh khah 好，伊 mā tsiok 想 beh 考榜首 hōo 馬修 kah 瑪俐有面子。

三禮拜過去，iu-guân 無消無息。

有一工安妮 uì 窗 á 去看 tiòh 黛娜 tsông 過來，手裡提一份報紙。

無 guā 久，伊就衝入來講：「安妮，你考 tiâu ah！而且是頭名！你 kah 萊義柏 lóng 是第一，m̄-koh 你 ê 名排 tī 頭一个。」

「真正 m̄ 敢相信，我進前想 beh 考頭名 ê 願望 tsiânn-sit 實現 ah。」

第十八章
獎學金

　　秋天開始安妮 ài 去皇后師範學院讀冊，大姑婆 kā 伊 tàu tshuē-tiȯh 宿舍 thang tuà，伊頭起先會心悶厝裡，好佳哉有茱安 hām 茹美 lóng 做伙 tī hia，tsit-má 看 tiȯh 派椒思伊 mā bē 棄嫌 ah。

　　禮拜時 á 安妮若 m̄ 是轉去厝就是去大姑婆 hia，後--來伊交 tiȯh 新朋友，就 khah 無 hiah-nī 想厝 ah。伊認真 phah-piànn 讀冊，目標是 ē-tàng 提 tiȯh 禮望（Redmond）大學提供 ê 兩種獎學金，一種是全校第一名 ê 獎學金，另外一種是大學全額 ê 獎學金，thìng 好免 lȧp 學費。

　　考試了後，學期成績 iáu-bē 宣佈進前，安妮 kah 茱安做伙 kiânn 路去學校 ê 時，安妮講：「我應該無才調提 tiòh 大學全額 ê 助學金，tàk-ke lóng 講稽瑁俐（Emily Clay）ê 機會較大面，我無 beh 去公佈欄看啥人贏，你去看了才 kā 我講，我若無 tiòh，請你好禮á kā 我講，mài hōo 我傷心，好 bô？」

　　茱安答應伊，tng in kiânn 入學校大廳，看 tiòh 一群查埔學生 kā 萊義柏扛起來 thènn kuân-kuân：「恭喜萊義柏提 tiòh 全校第一名！」

　　安妮 ê 心情眞沉重，伊竟然輸 hōo 萊義柏！伊知影馬修 tiānn-tiòh 會感覺 tsiok 無彩，馬修進前直直講安妮一定會提 tiòh 獎學金 ê。

　　Hiông-hiông，聽 tiòh 有人 leh huah-hiu：「恭喜施安妮提 tiòh 全額獎學金！」

　　所有 ê 查某學生 lóng tsáu 去 kā 安妮恭喜，安妮細聲 kā 茱安講：「馬修 kah 瑪俐一定會歡喜 kah！」

　　後--來，瑪俐 kah 馬修去參加安妮 tī 皇后師範學院 ê 畢業典禮，in 聽安妮朗讀 ka-kī 所寫 ê 文章 ê 時，感覺 tsiok 光榮。

　　馬修細聲問瑪俐：「你 tsit-má kám 有眞歡喜咱當初 kā 伊留落來？」

「這 m̄ 是我
第一 pái 感覺眞好
運。阿兄你眞 gâu kā
我 khau-sé neh！」

安妮 tuè 馬修 kah 瑪俐轉去亞檬
里 ê 時，黛娜已經 tī 靑瓦厝等伊 ah。

「啊，iáu 是轉來厝裡上好，ē-tàng 看 tiȯh 你 koh
khah 好！」安妮 kā 黛娜講。

「Tsit-má 你已經提 tiȯh 獎學金，kám 是 beh 開
始教冊 ah？」黛娜問安妮。

「無 neh，秋天 ê 時我 beh 去讀禮望大學，我
tsit-má beh 先好好 á 享受 tsit 三個月 ê 暑假！」

第二工食早頓 ê 時，安妮問瑪俐：「馬修有要緊
bô？伊看起來若像身體無 kài 爽快？」

「伊最近心臟無好，我 tsiok 煩惱伊。伊 siunn 過頭 piànn 勢，huān 勢你 tò 轉來 ah，伊 ē-tàng 歇一下，而且伊看 tiòh 你，精神 mā 會 ke 眞好。」

Hit 暗，安妮 tuè 馬修去後壁 ê 牧場牽牛轉來。

「你 siunn piànn 勢 ah，ài 好好 á 歇睏一下。」

「可能我定定會 bē 記得 ka-kī 已經有歲 ah。」

「我 tsit-má tian-tò tsiok 希望我是恁當初想 beh tih ê 查埔 gín-á，án-ne 我就 ē-tàng kā 你 tàu 跤手 ah。」

「有你 honnh，用十二个查埔 gín-á kah 我換，我 to 無 ài，因爲今年皇后師範學院 m̄ 是查埔 gín-á 提 tiòh 獎學金 neh，是一个查某 gín-á 喔，而且伊是我 ê 查某 kiánn neh！」

第十九章
艱苦 ê 時刻

「馬修！馬修！你是 án-tsuánn？你 kám 是人無爽快？」瑪俐大聲 hiu。

安妮聽 tiòh mā 趕緊 tsông 入來灶跤，m̄-koh in iáu-bē 趕到馬修 ê 身軀邊，馬修就昏 tó tī 塗跤 ah。

「安妮！緊 leh！緊 leh！緊去 tshuē 馬丁（Martin）！」

馬丁是 in tshiànn ê sin-lô，伊隨 piànn 去 tshuē 醫生，但是 bē-hù ah，馬修已經過身 ah。

Hit 暗，瑪俐聽 tiòh 安妮 tī 房間 leh háu，就去安慰伊。

瑪俐 kā 安妮 lám-tiâu-tiâu 講：「好 ah！M̄-thang koh háu ah，伊 bē koh tò 轉來 ah。」

「馬修無 tī leh ah，咱日子 beh án-tsuánn 過？」安妮 ná háu ná 講。

「咱 ài 互相倚靠。若無你，我 mā m̄ 知 beh án-tsuánn 過日。我 íng 過對你 khah 惡 khah 嚴格，你 ài 知影我 lóng 是因爲疼你、爲你好。自從你搬來了後，我 ê 生活 ke 眞快樂，你 gâu 讀冊 mā hōo 我感覺眞有榮光。」

兩工後，in kā 馬修 ê 後事圓滿，生活 mā tàuh-tàuh-á 恢復，只是安妮 iu-guân 眞 siàu 念馬修，定定會想 tiòh 伊。

一工暗時，瑪俐 kah 安妮做伙坐 tī 門跤口，瑪俐講：「醫生今 á 日有來，伊叫我明 á 載去鎮裡看眼科，希望伊 kā 我 hô 一副 hàh-su ê 目鏡。你 kám ē-tàng ka-kī tī 厝裡？」

「無問題，黛娜會來陪我，你免煩惱，我 bē koh 惹麻煩 ah！」

瑪俐笑 hai-hai 講：「你 kám 會記得 hit pái 你 kā 頭毛染做靑色？」

　　安妮笑笑 á 講:「我永遠 bē 放 bē 記得,因為我以前真正 tsiok 無佮意我 ê 紅頭毛 hām 雀斑,想 bē 到 tsit-má 雀斑 lóng 無--去 ah!Ta̍k-ke lóng o-ló 我 ê 頭毛是紅婍 á 紅婍,當然除了派椒思以外。」

　　隔轉工瑪俐去鎮裡 hōo 眼科醫生看,暗時 tò 轉來了後,面憂面 kat 坐 tī 食飯桌 hia。

　　安妮問:「你人是 m̄ 是無爽快?」

「無啦！眼科醫生講我 m̄-thang koh 看冊、thīnn 衫抑是做所有會用眼過多 ê 代誌，我若聽伊 ê 話，koh 掛伊 hô ê 目鏡，我 ê 目睭就 bē 害去，若無，koh 六個月我就會變 tshenn-mê。」

「你若 khah 注意 leh，你 ê 目睭就 bē 害去，而且 huān 勢新目鏡會 hōo 你頭殼 bē koh 疼。」

「我若 lóng bē-tàng 看冊、thīnn 衫、tshiah 膨紗，我是 iáu ē-tàng 做啥物？我 kah tshenn-mê 有啥物精差？」

瑪俐去睏了後，安妮坐 tī 窗 á 邊想看 beh án-tsuánn 幫助瑪俐，無一時 á 久，伊就 tshuē-tio̍h 答案 ah。

第二十章
永遠 ê 青瓦厝

　　過幾工 á，安妮看 tiòh 瑪俐 tī 門口埕 kah 一个查埔人 leh 講話，講 suah 轉來 ê 時目 khoo 紅紅講：「伊想 beh 買咱 ê 農場。」

　　「買咱 ê 農場！你 beh 賣農場？」安妮驚一 tiô。

　　「無法度啊！」講 suah，伊目屎就 liàn 落來。「我無才調 ka-kī 一个人顧規个農場，尤其是萬不二我若目睭 tshenn-mê leh？我自來 to 無想 tiòh 講有一工我會 kā 厝賣掉……。」

「你 bē-tàng kā 青瓦厝賣掉！」

「我 mā 無 ài，m̄-koh 我無法度 ka-kī 一个留 tiàm tsia。」瑪俐 ná 講 ná háu。

「你 bē ka-kī 一个 tī tsia 啊！我已經決定無 beh 去讀禮望大學 ah，我會陪你。」

「無 beh 去讀禮望大學！你是 leh 講啥物？」瑪俐 giah 頭起來看伊。

「就像我講 ê，我會放棄獎學金。你去看眼科醫生轉來 hit 暗，我就決定 ah。想 tio̍h tsit 幾冬來你 tsiah-nī 疼惜我，我絕對 bē 放你孤單一个人。」

安妮 kā 瑪俐 ê 手牽起來講：「我 kā 你講我 ê 計畫。白先生明年想 beh suè 咱 ê 農場，所以你免煩惱農場。」安妮繼續講：「我會去佳模知（Carmody）國小教，若下班轉來，暗時會 kah 你做伴、唸冊 hōo 你聽。我本來是想 beh 去亞檬里國小，m̄-koh 萊義柏已經 ín beh 去 hia ah。」

「你 m̄ 是想 beh 讀大學？」

「我按算 tī 厝裡 ka-kī 讀，mā huān 勢有一工我就 ē-tàng 去禮望大學讀冊。現此時上重要 ê 是處理農場 ê 代誌 kah 照顧你。」

「我應該 ài 堅持 hōo 你去讀大學才 tiòh，只是眼前我真正有困難，所以 tsit 句話就免 ke 講 ah。後過我一定會想辦法 hōo 你完成 tsit 个願望。」

有一暗藺太太來 kā in 講一个消息：「教育局已經決定欲派安妮去亞檬里國小教。」

「Kám m̄ 是萊義柏 beh 去？」

「本來是伊 beh 去無 m̄-tiòh，m̄-koh 伊一下聽 tiòh 講你想 beh 去亞檬里國小，thang 好 tsiū 近照顧瑪俐，伊就 kā in 推薦你，ka-kī 自願去白沙鎮教冊。」

「Án-ne 我 kám ài 接受？ Hōo 萊義柏爲 tiòh 我來犧牲 kám 好？」

「已經決定 ah。伊已經 kah 白沙國小簽約，你 tsit-má 講你無 ài 去亞檬里國小 mā 無 khah-tsuàh ah，不如就大大方方 kā 接受。」

第二工黃昏 ê 時，安妮 bán 花去探馬修 ê 墓，tò 轉去 ê 半路遇 tiòh 萊義柏，萊義柏 iàt 帽 á kah 伊 sio-tsioh-mn̄g，本來萊義柏 ná iàt 就 beh kiânn 過去，安妮 suah 停落來 kah 伊握手。

安妮規个面紅 kòng-kòng 講：「我一定 ài kā 你 sueh 多謝，眞感謝你 kā 學校讓 hōo 我，你 tsiah-nī 好心，我 tsiok 感心 neh ！」

萊義柏真熱誠握安妮 ê 手講：「我真歡喜 kā 你 tàu-sann-kāng，咱以後 kám ē-tàng 做朋友？你 kám tsiânn-sit 原諒我 ah？」

安妮笑笑 á 講：「其實你 kò 船來解救我 hit 工我就原諒你 ah，只是我 hit 陣 iáu m̄ 承認 niā-niā，後--來我一直真後悔。」

萊義柏 mā 笑笑 á 講：「咱會變做上好 ê 朋友，咱應該就是註定 beh 做好朋友 ê。來！我陪你 kiânn 轉去。」

安妮入去灶跤 ê 時，瑪俐真好 hiân 講：「Tú-tsiah 是啥物人 kah 你 tī 外口 leh 講話？」

「是萊義柏，我 tī 路裡 tú-tio̍h 伊。」

「我 m̄ 知影恁兩个人交情 tsiah-nī 好，ē-tàng tī 門跤口講半點鐘。」瑪俐微微 á 笑。

「阮真正有講半點鐘久 hiooh？我 lia̍h-tsún 才講幾分鐘 á niā-niā。是講，阮有五冬 ê 時間無講過話，tsit-má 補一下 mā 是應該 ê。」

安妮 hit 暗 tī 窗 á 邊坐 tsiok 久，一陣風 kā 外口 ê 櫻桃樹 hām 蘋果樹吹 kah 搖來幌去，雲杉頂 ê 天星閃閃 sih-sih，伊看會 tio̍h 遠遠黛娜房間 ê 電火。

安妮對未來充滿信心，伊一方面 ná 教冊 ná 進修，一方面 thìng 好 kah tsē-tsē 好朋友 tàu 陣。

　　上重要 ê 是，青瓦厝是伊 kah 瑪俐永遠 ê 家。

Anne

of

Green Gables

Lucy Maud Montgomery

Chapter 1

The Beginning

One warm June afternoon, Mrs. Lynde looked out of her kitchen window and happened to see Matthew Cuthbert drive by in a horse and buggy.

Mrs. Lynde thought to herself: "Matthew is so quiet and shy that he seldom talks to others. Why is he wearing his best suit? Where is he going? Let me go over and investigate."

Mrs. Lynde enjoyed sticking her nose into everyone's business in Avonlea. She figured that she could go visit his sister, Marilla Cuthbert, who lived at Green Gables with Matthew.

When Mrs. Lynde stepped in, Marilla was busy in the kitchen. She was tall and thin; her dark hair had gray streaks and was twisted into a hard knot at the back of her head.

Marilla said, "Hi, Rachel. Won't you sit down? What has brought you here this afternoon?"

Mrs. Lynde, "I just saw Matthew driving off. It got me worried that you were sick, so he had to go get the doctor."

Rachael replied, "Oh, no, I'm fine. We are getting a boy from an orphanage in Nova Scotia, and he is coming on the train this afternoon. Matthew went to Bright River station to pick him up."

Mrs. Lynde couldn't believe what she just heard! The Cuthberts were adopting a boy! The world was certainly turning upside down! She said, "Are you serious?"

Marilla answered, "Of course. You know I don't joke around. Matthews is getting up in years, and he's not as strong as he once was. He needs a boy to help him on the farm."

Mrs. Lyde would have liked to stay until Matthew came back with the boy, but it'd have taken at least two hours. So she decided to go tell Mrs. Bell this surprising news. When she was out in the lane, she said, "I am sorry for that poor orphan boy, the Cuthberts know nothing about raising children!"

When Matthew reached the station, there was no sign of any train. There was only a little girl sitting by herself at the end of the long platform.

The station-master was locking up the ticket office, so Matthew asked him, "Excuse me, sir. Will the five thirty train arrive soon?"

The station master replied, "It had been in and gone. But a girl got off and asked for you."

Matthew muttered to himself, "That's not right. It should be a boy not a girl."

The station master said, "Well, you'd better talk to her. She's been waiting for some time."

The little girl was wearing an ugly yellowish-gray dress. Beneath her faded brown sailor hat were two thick red braids that hung in front of her. Her face was small, thin and freckled; her huge gray-green eyes looked intently at him.

She said to Matthew, "I suppose you are Mr. Cuthbert of Green Gables? I was afraid that you weren't coming for me. If you didn't, I had made up my mind I'd climb up to that tree to sleep. Don't you think it'd be lovely to sleep in a tree all white with moonlight?"

Matthew looked into the girl's glowing eyes and knew that he couldn't tell her there had been a mistake. He had to take her home tonight. "I'm sorry I was late. Come along. Give me your bag."

The girl said, "Oh, I can carry it. It isn't heavy, though it's got all my worldly goods in it."

Matthew helped her get on the buggy, and she said, "It's wonderful that I'm going to live with you! Were you ever in an orphanage? It's worse than anything, because there's little scope for any imagination, believe me!" The girl kept talking all the way back to Avonlea. Matthew enjoyed her chatter and found himself liking this lively girl.

They drove up a hill, and turned at a bend. At the valley down below were some farm houses. "That's Green Gables, isn't it?" the girl said, pointing.

Matthew nodded and said, "Well, you've guessed it."

The girl sighed with content, "I was worried it was all a dream. But it's real! We're nearly home!"

Chapter 2

A Mistake

They finally arrived at Green Gables. Marilla came forward as Matthew opened the door. She was surprised to see the girl and asked, "Matthew, who is that? Where's the boy?"

Matthew muttered, "There wasn't any boy. There was only her."

Marilla said, "But we asked for a boy, not a girl."

Matthew, "They only sent a girl. I had to bring her home. I couldn't leave her alone at the station."

"You don't want me!" the girl cried. "I should've known it's all too beautiful to last. Why would anyone ever want me?" She sat down on the kitchen chair and started crying.

Marilla, "Well, there's no need to cry about it!"

The girl said with a tear-stained face, "Yes, there is need! This is the most tragic thing that has ever happened to me!"

Marilla had to stifle her smile and asked, "Don't cry any more. We won't send you back tonight. What's your name?"

The girl stopped sobbing, hesitated for a moment and answered, "Will you please call me Cordelia?"

Marilla found it strange and asked, "Is that your name?"

The girl admitted, "No-o-o, not exactly. My real name is Anne Shirley. Everyone calls me Anne. But I prefer Cordelia, it's so much more romantic!"

Marilla said, "Fiddlesticks! Anne is a good sensible name."

The girl said, "If you call me Anne, please spell it with an 'e'? It's so much nicer than just dreadful A-n-n."

"Very well, then. Anne spelled with an 'e', can you tell me how this mistake came to be made?"

"Mrs. Spencer said distinctly that you wanted a girl about eleven years old. There's a little girl named Lily Jones. She's really pretty so Mrs. Spencer kept her for herself. Would you keep me if I were pretty?"

Marilla, "No. We need a boy to help Matthew on the farm. A girl would be of no use to us."

They sat down to supper, but Anne just nibbled at her food.

Matthew said, "I guess she's tired. Best put her to bed, Marilla."

Marilla took Anne to the east gable bedroom. The walls were bare and white. The floor was bare too, except for a round braided mat in the middle. There was a bed in one corner of the room.

With a sob, Anne slipped on a faded nightgown and jumped

on the bed. Then she pulled the covers over her head.

Marilla said, "Good night, then."

Anne's small pale face and big eyes appeared over the covers. She said, "How can you call it a good night when you know it must be the very worst night I've ever had?" Then she dived down under the covers again.

Marilla went back down to the kitchen and told Matthew, "This girl will have to be sent back to the orphanage."

Matthew, "But she's a real nice little thing. It'll be a pity to send her back. She's set on staying here."

Marilla stared at Matthew. "You don't mean to say we ought to keep her! What good would she be to us?"

Matthew, "We might be some good to her. Or she can be company for you."

Marilla, "I don't need company, and I'm not going to keep her."

Matthew, "It's just as you say, of course. I'm going to bed."

Marilla did the dishes and went to bed, too. Upstairs in the east gable, a lonely girl cried herself to sleep.

Chapter 3

Anne's Past

Anne woke up the next morning, confused about where she was. Then she remembered that she was at Green Gables, but they didn't want her just because she was a girl!

Anne jumped off bed, knelt on the floor and looked out. The house was flanked by apple trees and cherry trees on each side. Lilac trees were bursting with purple flowers in the garden. Below the garden was a green field sloping down to a brook. Beyond it was a hill green with spruce and fir.

Then, Marilla placed her hand on Anne's shoulder, startling her.

She told Anne, "It's time to get dressed."

Anne stood up and said, "Green Gables is so beautiful. I was just imagining living here forever."

Marilla said, "Get dressed and have breakfast now. Stop your imagining."

When Anne came downstairs, her dress was neatly on, her face was clean, and her hair was brushed and braided.

After breakfast, Marilla asked, "Do you know how to wash dishes properly?"

Anne, "No problem. In fact, I'm better at looking after little children. It's a pity you don't have any little children for me to look after."

Marilla, "I don't want any more children than I've got now! I don't know what's to be done with you. Matthew is a silly man."

Anne, "I think he's lovely! As soon as I saw him, I knew he was a kindred spirit!"

Marilla, "You're both queer, that's all I'm saying. Go wash the dishes now. Use enough hot water, and dry them well."

After she was done, Marilla told Anne that she could go out and play.

Anne dashed toward the door. However, she stopped right in front of the door, came back and sat down by the kitchen table.

Marilla, "What's the matter now?"

Anne, "I don't dare go out. I can't help loving all the flowers, trees, the orchard and the brook. I was so glad when I thought I was going to live here, with all these beautiful things to love. Sadly, my dream has been shattered. It won't matter if I look at them now, so I might as well sit here."

Anne stayed in the kitchen until Matthew came back for lunch. Marilla said during their meal, " I'll take Anne to White Sands to Mrs. Spencer, and she should be able to make arrangements to send Anne back to the orphanage."

Matthew stayed silent the whole time. Once he was done eating, he got the buggy ready, and opened the gate to the front yard to let Marilla and Anne out. Marilla looked back at Matthew, who leaned by the gate, looking devastated.

Anne, "I've made up my mind to enjoy this drive and not think about the orphanage. Will we pass by the Lake of Shining Waters?"

Marilla, "We're not going over Berry's pond, if that's what you mean. We're going by the shore road."

Anne said, "Shore road sounds romantic. White Sands is a pretty name too, but I don't like it as well as Avonlea, which sounds like music!"

Marilla replied, "Since you've been talking nonstop, you might as well tell me about yourself."

Anne, " I was born in Nova Scotia, and will turn twelve soon. My father was Walter Shirley, and my mother was Bertha Shirley. They were both school teachers, but they both passed away when I was an infant. Because I didn't have any relatives, nobody knew what to do with me. Finally Mrs. Thomas took me in. Mrs. Thomas used to do house cleaning for my parents, and she had four kids who needed a lot of looking after. So once I got a bit older, it was my turn to take care of them. Unfortunately, Mr. Thomas passed away when I was eight. His mother took Mrs. Thomas and the four kids, but she didn't want me."

"What happened later?"

"Then Mrs. Hammond said she'd take me, seeing I was handy with children. She had eight kids, and six of them were twins. When Mr. Hammond died, she and the kids moved away, so I had to go to the orphanage. They were overcrowded, but they had to take me."

"Were those women good to you?"

"O-o-o-h," Anne's face turned red with embarrassment. "Oh, they meant to be. They had a lot to worry about, and they were very poor. Plus, Mrs. Thomas' husband got drunk a lot."

Marilla asked no more questions. Pity was stirring in her heart. What a terrible life she had had. No wonder she longed for a real home. What if she let Anne stay? Matthew was set on it, and she seemed a rather nice girl.

Chapter 4

An Important Decision

Marilla and Anne arrived at Mrs. Spencer's house. Mrs. Spencer was surprised to see them, saying, "You're the last folks I was expecting today! How are you, Anne?"

Anne quietly answered, "I'm fine. Thank you."

Marilla said, "There has been a mistake. We told Robert that we wanted a boy, but why do we get a girl instead?"

Mrs. Spencer answered, "You don't say! His daughter said you wanted a girl."

"Now that the mistake has been made, can we send her back to the orphanage?" Marilla said.

"I suppose so. But Mrs. Blewett said she needed a little girl to help her. She has a large family, and Anne can be the very girl for her," said Mrs. Spencer.

Marilla had never met Mrs. Blewett in person, but had heard that she was mean and stingy. Also, several servant girls told terrifying tales of her children. Marilla felt uneasy about handing Anne over to such a family.

"There comes Mrs. Blewett!" Mrs. Spencer said, "How lucky! Let's settle the matter right away."

Mrs. Spencer invited Mrs. Blewett to the living room, and told Anne to sit on the stool at the corner.

Staring at the sharp-faced Mrs. Blewett, Anne clasped her hands tightly. Was she going to be given to this mean-looking woman? Anxiety and fear brought tears to her eyes.

Mrs. Spencer explained to Mrs. Blewett about the mistake, and said, "Earlier you said you needed a girl to help you. I think she'll be the right one for you."

Mrs. Blewett looked at Anne from head to toe, and said to Anne, "If I take you, you have to be a good girl, you know—good and smart and respectful. I'll expect you to earn your keep, and no mistake about that. "

Mrs. Blewett told Marilla, "I suppose I'll take her off your hands. If you like, I can take her right away."

Marilla knew she couldn't hand Anne over to such a woman, so she said slowly, "Well, I don't know. Matthew and I may still want to keep Anne. I just came over to find out how the mistake had occurred. I think I'd better take her home again."

Then, they climbed back into the buggy.

"Did you really say that perhaps you would let me stay at Green Gables? Or did I only imagine that you did?"Anne asked.

"I think you'd better learn to control that imagination of yours," Marilla said. "It isn't decided yet."

"I'll do anything you want if you keep me," Anne said meekly.

When they arrived back at Green Gables, Marilla told Matthew what had happened.

"I wouldn't give a dog I liked to that Blewett woman. Not to mention Anne!" said Matthew.

Marilla admitted that she didn't like Mrs. Blewett's style either. She said, "Since you seem to want to keep Anne, then I suppose I'm willing."

The next day, Marilla told Anne that she could stay.

"Thank you! I'm as happy as a clam! But what should I call you?" Anne said.

"You'll call me just plain Marilla. I'm not used to being called Miss Cuthbert, and it would make me nervous."

"It sounds disrespectful to just say Marilla," said Anne.

"Not if you speak respectfully. Everyone in Avonlea calls me Marilla."

Anne asked another question, "Do you think that I'll have a bosom friend in Avonlea? I've dreamed of meeting her all my life."

"Diana Barry lives nearby and she's about your age. She's a very nice little girl. You have to be careful how you behave yourself, though. Mrs. Barry won't let Diana play with any girl who isn't nice and good."

Anne's eyes glowed with interest. "What is Diana like? I hope her hair isn't red. It's bad enough to have red hair myself, but I couldn't endure it in a bosom friend," she said.

Marilla answered, "Diana is a very pretty little girl. She has black eyes and hair and rosy cheeks. And she is good and smart, which is better than being pretty."

"Oh, I'm so glad she's pretty," said Anne. I know I'm not pretty myself, so it'd be wonderful to have a beautiful bosom friend."

Before bed, it occurred to Anne that she needed to say prayers. She sat in a chair by the window, and said, " I'm going to imagine that I am tall and beautiful, dressed in a white lace gown. There are pearls in my black hair."

She ran to the mirror and peered into it. Her freckled face and gray eyes looked back at her.

Anne said to herself, "You're only plain Anne of Green Gables. But it's a million times nicer to be Anne of Green Gables than Anne of nowhere, isn't it?"

Chapter 5

Going to Church

"Well, how do you like them?" asked Marilla.

Looking at the new dresses that Marilla made, Anne said quietly, "I'll imagine that I like them."

"I don't want you to imagine it," said Marilla, offended. "Oh, I can see that you don't like the dresses. What's the matter with them?"

"They're—they're not—pretty," said Anne reluctantly.

"Pretty!" Marilla sniffed. "Those are good, sensible dresses without frills or ruffles. The brown gingham and the blue print will do for school. The black-and-white checkered sateen is for church and Sunday school. I'll expect you to keep them neat and clean. I should think you'd be grateful to get them after those ragged things you've been wearing."

"Oh, I'm grateful," Anne said. "But I wish to wear just a dress with puff sleeves. Puffed sleeves are so fashionable now."

"Well, I think they look ridiculous. I prefer plain and sensible dresses. Now hang those dresses up carefully, and then sit down and learn the Sunday-school lesson for tomorrow."

Marilla disappeared downstairs. Anne looked at the dresses

and sighed. "I did hope there would be a white dress with puffed sleeves," she whispered. "Well, I can imagine that one of them has lace frills and three puffed sleeves."

The next morning, Marilla had a headache so she couldn't take Anne to Sunday school. "You have to go with Mrs. Lynde," she said. "Now, behave yourself. Don't stare at people and don't fidget. Here's a cent for collection."

Anne started off down the lane. She picked buttercups and wild roses along the way. She made a heavy wreath of pink and yellow flowers and put it on her new plain sailor hat. Anne thought the flowers would make her look prettier. When she reached Mrs. Lynde's house, she wasn't home. So Anne went to the church alone.

Since Anne's flowers had faded, she discarded the wreath in the lane on the way back.

"Well, how did you like Sunday school?" Marilla wanted to know.

"I didn't like it a bit. It was horrid."

"Anne Shirley!" Marilla exclaimed.

"Mr. Bell made an awfully long prayer," Anne said. "And all the girls in my class had puffed sleeves except for me."

"You shouldn't have been thinking about your sleeves in Sunday school. You should have been attending to the lesson."

"Oh, yes. I answered a lot of questions. After Sunday school, I asked Miss Rogerson to show me your pew. The sermon was awfully long, too. The minister wasn't a bit interesting, so I didn't listen to him very much."

Deep down, Marilla secretly agreed with what Anne had said about the minister's sermons and Mr. Bell's prayers. She knew she should scold Anne, but she just couldn't bring herself to do it.

The next Friday, Marilla visited Mrs. Lynde and heard about the flower-wreath hat.

"Anne," Marilla said, "Mrs. Lynde says you went to church with roses and buttercups on your hat? That was very silly!"

"But lots of girls had flowers pinned on their dresses."

"Don't answer me back, Anne." Marilla snapped. "Mrs. Lynde says people said it was dreadful. They'd think I had no better sense then to let you go out to church like that."

"Oh, I'm so sorry," said Anne, with tears welling into her eyes. "I never thought you would mind. Lots of the girls had flowers on their hats. Maybe you'd better send me back to the orphanage. That would be terrible, but it would be better than being a trial to you."

"Nonsense," said Marilla. "I don't want to send you back to the orphanage. All I want is that you should behave like other little girls. Don't cry any more. I've got some good news for you. Diana Berry came home this afternoon. I'm going up to see if I can borrow a skirt pattern from Mrs. Berry, and would you like to come with me to meet Diana?"

Anne stood up and clasped her hands. "Oh, Marilla, I'm frightened," she said. "What if she doesn't like me?"

Marilla said, "I think Diana will like you. It's her mother that you've got to impress. I hope she hasn't heard about the flowers on your hat; otherwise, she won't know what to think of you. You must be polite and well-behaved, and don't say anything startling."

Chapter 6

A New Friend

Anne and Marilla went over to Orchard Slope farm. Mrs. Barry came to the door in answer to Marilla's knock. She was tall with black hair and black eyes.

"How do you do, Marilla," she said. "Come in. And this is the little girl you have adopted, I suppose?"

"Yes, this is Anne Shirley," Marilla said.

Mrs. Barry shook Anne's hands and kindly asked, "How are you?"

"I'm well in body, but rumpled in spirit. Thank you, ma'am." She said and turned to Marilla, whispering, "That wasn't startling, was it?"

Diana was sitting on the sofa reading a book. When Marilla and Anne entered, she dropped the book and smiled at them.

"This is my little girl, Diana," said Mrs. Barry. "Diana, why don't you take Anne out into the garden and show her your flowers?"

Anne and Diana went out to the garden. They gazed shyly at each other over a clump of tiger lilies.

"Oh, Diana," said Anne at last, "do you think...you can like me a little...enough to be my bosom friend?"

Diana laughed and said, "I guess so. I'm awfully glad that you've come to live at Green Gables. It'll be fun to have someone to play with. My sisters are not old enough."

"Will you vow to be my bosom friend forever and ever?" asked Anne eagerly.

"Sure, I don't mind doing it. How do you do it?" asked Diana.

"We must hold hands—so," Anne said gravely. "I solemnly vow to be faithful to my bosom friend, Diana Barry, as long as the sun and the moon shall endure. Now you say it and put my name in it."

Diana repeated the vow with a giggle. Then she said, "You're a funny girl, Anne. But I'm going to like you very much."

When Marilla and Anne went home, Diana went with them as far as the brook. They promised to spend the next afternoon together.

Anne told Marilla, "I'm the happiest girl on Prince Edward Island! We're going to build a playhouse together tomorrow. Diana is going to lend me a book to read and teach me to sing a song. I wish I had something to give Diana. Did you know that I'm an inch taller than her? But she is ever so much fatter; she says she'd like to be thin, but I think she said it to make me feel better."

"Well, I hope you won't talk Diana to death," Marilla said. "And remember this, Anne. You're not going to play all the time. You'll have your chores to do and it'll have to be done first."

Once they got back to Green Gables, Matthew had a surprise for Anne. He pulled a small bag from his pocket and handed it to her. "I heard you say you liked chocolate candies, so I got you some," he said.

"Humph," sniffed Marilla. "It'll ruin her teeth and stomach. There, there, child, don't look so miserable. You can eat those, since Matthew has gone and got them. Don't get sick eating them all at once."

"Oh, I won't," said Anne. "I'll just eat one tonight. And I can give Diana half of them, can't I? The other half will taste twice as sweet to me if I give her some. I'm happy I have something to give her."

"I will say it for the child," said Marilla when Anne had gone to bed. "She isn't stingy. I'm glad. Dear me, it's only three weeks since she came, and it seems as if she'd been here always. I can't imagine this place without her. I admit that I'm getting fond of her. Now, don't be looking I told-you-so, Matthew!"

Chapter 7

Going to School

School started in September. The Avonlea School was a whitewashed building with one big room and desks that opened and shut at the top.

Anne came home and told Marilla, "I think I'm going to like school. I made friends with Ruby Gillis and Tillie Boutler. But I still like Diana best and always will. And Prissy Andrews told Sara Gillis that I had a very pretty nose. That is the first compliment I have ever had about my looks. Do I have a pretty nose?"

"Your nose is nice enough," Marilla said shortly. Secretly she thought Anne's nose was remarkably pretty.

Three weeks later, Anne and Diana were walking to school. Diana said, "Gilbert Blythe will be in school today. He's been visiting his cousins all summer. He didn't go to school for several years when he went out west with his father. He's in sixth grade even though he's almost fourteen!"

They walked into the classroom and sat at the desk they shared.

"That's Gilbert Blythe sitting right across from you," whispered Diana. "Don't you think he's handsome?"

Anne looked across the aisle. Gilbert Blythe was a tall boy

with curly brown hair and a teasing smile. He turned his head and winked at Anne.

"He is handsome," Anne whispered to Diana, "but I think he's very bold. It isn't good manners to wink at a stranger."

But it was not until the afternoon that things really began to happen.

Mr. Phillips was back in the corner of the room explaining a math problem to Prissy Andrews, and the rest of the class was doing as they pleased. They were eating apples, drawing pictures and whispering.

Gilbert Blythe was trying to make Anne look at him; but she was gazing out the window, daydreaming.

Gilbert Blythe wasn't used to being ignored by girls. So he picked up Anne's long red braid. Then he said in a piercing whisper, "Carrots! Carrots!"

Anne jumped to her feet, staring at him. " How dare you!" she shouted.

And then—Thwack! Anne hit Gilbert over the head with her slate, cracking it.

Mr. Phillips stalked down the aisle. "Anne Shirley, what is the meaning of this?" he asked angrily.

Anne didn't reply. She wouldn't tell the whole class she had been called "carrots."

"It was my fault, Mr. Phillips. I teased her," Gilbert explained.

Mr. Phillips paid no attention to Gilbert. "I'm sorry to see a student of mine display such a temper," he said. "Anne, go stand in front of the blackboard."

Anne did not cry or hang her head, because anger was still too hot in her heart.

After school, Anne marched out with her head held high. Gilbert Blythe hurried behind, and apologized, "I'm sorry I made fun of your hair, Anne. Honest, please don't be mad."

But Anne swept by without looking at him.

"Oh, how could you, Anne?" Diana said as they went down the road.

"I shall never forgive Gilbert Blythe," Anne said firmly.

"But Gilbert makes fun of all the girls," Diana said. "He laughs at my hair because it's so black. He even calls me a crow."

"Being called carrots is worse," said Anne. "Gilbert Blythe has hurt my feelings deeply, Diana."

But this was just the beginning.

Chapter 8

Gilbert Blythe

The next day, Mr. Phillips told his class, "You have been coming back from lunch late. You have to be in your seats when I return."

At lunchtime, everyone went to Mr. Bell's spruce grove. Anne was in the far end of the grove, wandering and singing happily to herself.

Suddenly Jimmy Glover shouted, "Master's coming!"

The girls reached the schoolhouse just in time, but the boys were late because they had to climb down from the trees. Anne ran fast like a deer and caught up with the boys at the door. They swept into the room when Mr. Phillips hung up his hat.

Anne dropped into her seat, gasping for breath.

Mr. Phillips didn't want to punish twelve students for being late, but he had to punish someone.

"Anne Shirley," he said, "since you seem to be so fond of the boys' company, I shall let you have more. Go sit with Gilbert Blythe."

The other boys snickered. Diana turned pale, and Anne stared at her teacher.

"Did you hear what I said, Anne?" asked Mr. Phillips.

"Yes, sir," said Anne slowly. "But I didn't think you really meant it."

"I assure you I did," said Mr. Phillips sternly.

For a moment, Anne looked as if she meant to disobey. Then she stood up and stepped across the aisle. She sat down beside Gilbert Blythe and buried her face in her arms on the desk.

The other children whispered, giggled and nudged. Eventually, they returned to their own tasks.

When nobody was looking, Gilbert took from his desk a little pink candy heart with words on it, "You are sweet," and slipped it under the curve of Anne's arm.

When Anne raised her head, she took the pink heart between her fingertips and dropped it on the floor. She crushed the heart with the heel of her shoe, and then buried her face in her arms again.

When school went out, Anne marched to her desk, took out everything inside, including her books, writing tablet, pen and ink and arithmetic. Then she piled them neatly on her cracked slate.

"Why are you taking those things home, Anne?" Diana wanted to know as soon as they were out on the road.

"I am not coming back to school," said Anne.

Diana stared at Anne and asked, "Will Marilla let you stay home?"

"She'll have to," said Anne. "I'll never go to school again!"

"Oh, Anne! What shall I do? Mr. Phillips will make me sit with that terrible Gertie Pye. I know he will because she's sitting alone. Do come back, please!"

"I'd do almost anything in the world for you, Diana," said Anne sadly. "But I can't do this, so please don't ask me."

"Just think of all the fun you'll miss," said Diana. "We're going to play ball next week, and you've never played ball before. It's very exciting! And we're going to learn a new song. And we're all going to read a new book out loud by the brook. You love to read out loud, Anne."

But Anne's mind was made up. She would not go to school to Mr. Phillips again, which she told Marilla when she got home.

"Nonsense," said Marilla.

"It isn't nonsense at all, "said Anne. "Don't you understand? I have been insulted."

"Insulted fiddlesticks! You'll go to school tomorrow as usual!"

"Oh no," Anne shook her head. "I'm not going back. I'll learn my lessons at home and I'll be as good as I can be. But I will not go back to school!"

Marilla decided not to say anymore about school just then. Instead, she turned to Mrs. Lynde for her advice.

"Well," Mrs. Lynde said, "I'd let her stay at home for a little while, that's what I'd do. She'll cool off and be ready to go back on her own. The less fuss made the better, in my opinion."

Marilla took Mrs. Lynde's advice and not another word was said to Anne about going back to school. Anne learned her lessons at home, did her chores, and played with Diana when she got off school.

But Anne had made up her mind to hate Gilbert Blythe to the end of her life.

Chapter 9

The First Tea Party

"I'm going to a meeting this afternoon," Marilla said to Anne one Saturday morning in October. "If you want, you can ask Diana to come over and spend the afternoon and have tea here."

"Oh, thank you, Marilla!" Anne said happily. "I've longed to have Diana over for tea."

"You can open the little jar of cherry preserves and have it with fruit cake and cookies," Marilla said. "There's a bottle half-full of raspberry cordial that was left over from our church social. It's on the second shelf of the living room closet. You and Diana can have it if you like."

After Marilla had driven off, Diana came over. She was wearing her second best dress, just like a lady.

Anne also dressed in her second best and opened the front door primly. Both girls shook hands as if they had never met before. Diana put her hat down and they sat in the living room.

"How is your mother?" Anne asked, sounding all grown-up.

"She's very well, thank you. Is Mr. Cuthbert hauling potatoes to the ship this afternoon?" Diana said.

"Yes, our potato crop is very good this year. I hope your

father's crop is good, too."

"It is fairly good, thank you. Have you picked many apples yet?"

"Oh, ever so many," said Anne, forgetting to act grown-up and jumped up quickly. "Let's go out to the orchard and get the rest on the tree."

They picked and ate apples until Diana started talking about Gilbert. Anne didn't want to hear about him, so she jumped up and said they should go in and have some raspberry cordial.

Anne looked a while and finally found a bottle marked 'raspberry cordial' at the back of the top shelf. Anne put it on a tray and set it on the table with a glass.

"Help yourself, Diana," said Anne. "I don't want any after all those apples."

Diana poured herself a big glass of cordial, sipped it and said, "It's awfully good, Anne. I didn't know raspberry cordial was so nice."

"I'm very glad you like it. Take as much as you want," said Anne.

Diana drank a second big glass of cordial, and she drank a third.

"This cordial is so much nicer than Mrs. Lynde's. It doesn't taste a bit like hers."

"Of course Marilla's so much nicer. She's a famous cook. She's trying to teach me, but I'm a trial to her. One time I found a mouse drowned in the plum pudding sauce! I took it out, but I forgot to ask Marilla what to do with it until she brought it to the table. I remembered the mouse, and I shrieked out, 'Don't use that sauce! There was a mouse drowned in it!' And we had company that day! Why, Diana, what is the matter?"

Diana stood up unsteadily, and then she sat down again, putting her hands to her head. "I'm—I'm awfully sick," she said. "I—I—must go right home."

"Oh, but you can't go home without having tea!"

"I'm awfully sick. I must go home."

Anne got Diana's hat and went with her as far as the Barry yard fence. Then she cried all the way back to Green Gables. Her first tea party had been a total disaster!

Chapter 10

Mrs. Barry Got Angry

The next day was Sunday and the rain poured down all day, so Anne couldn't hang out with Diana. Monday afternoon, Marilla sent her down to Mrs. Lynde's on an errand.

Soon Anne came flying back up the lane, with tears streaming down her face. She dashed into the kitchen and flung herself on the sofa.

"Whatever has gone wrong now, Anne?" Marilla asked.

Anne sat up. "Mrs. Lynde went to see Mrs. Barry today," Anne sobbed. "Mrs. Barry said I got Diana drunk Saturday. She said I'm a bad little girl and she would never let Diana play with me again!"

Marilla stared in amazement and said, "Got her drunk! What on earth did you give her to drink?"

"Only raspberry cordial," Diana wailed. "I never thought raspberry cordial would get people drunk."

"Fiddlesticks!" said Marilla, marching to the living room pantry. There on the shelf was a bottle marked 'Raspberry Cordial.'

It was the bottle Marilla had used for her homemade currant wine. Marilla remembered that she had put the bottle of raspberry cordial down in the cellar instead of in the pantry as she had told Anne.

She went back to the kitchen, chuckling in spite of herself.

"Anne, you certainly know how to get yourself in trouble. You gave Diana currant wine instead of raspberry cordial. Didn't you know the difference yourself?"

"I never tasted it," said Anne. "Oh, what should I do now, Marilla? Mrs. Barry believes that I did it on purpose."

"There, there, child, don't cry. You were not to blame. You'd better go up this evening and tell her how it was."

"I don't think I could face Diana's mother," Anne sighed. "I wish you'd go, Marilla. She might listen to you."

"Well, I will." Said Marilla. "Don't cry anymore, Anne. It'll be alright."

But it wasn't alright. Anne could tell that from Marilla's face when she got home.

"Mrs. Barry won't forgive me, right?" Anne asked sadly.

"Mrs. Barry indeed!" snapped Marilla. "Of all the unreasonable women I ever saw, she's the worst. I told her it was a mistake and you weren't to blame, but she simply didn't believe me." Then, she whisked into the kitchen.

Marilla slipped into Anne's room that night and found that

Anne had cried herself to sleep.

"Poor little soul," Marilla murmured, lifting a loose curl of hair from Anne's tear-stained face. Then she bent down and kissed Anne's flushed check.

The next morning, Anne came down from her room with her books and slate on her arm.

"I'm going back to school," she announced. "That's all there is left for me now that my friend has been torn from me."

Marilla was surprised, but delighted about the situation.

Anne was welcomed back to school with open arms. Ruby Gillis passed three plums over to her. Ella May gave her an enormous paper pansy. Katie Boutler gave her an empty bottle to keep perfume in.

The girls were not the only ones who appreciated her. After lunch, Anne found on her desk a big apple. Anne was ready to take a bite, when she remembered that that kind of apple only grew in the Blythe orchard. It must have been left by her number-one enemy—Gilbert Blythe!

Anne dropped the apple as if it were a red-hot coal and wiped her fingers on her handkerchief.

All in all, Anne was happy to be back at school with her friends. However, she had to sit with Minnie Andrews, and she missed Diana terribly.

"Diana might have smiled at me once, I think," Anne told Marilla that night.

The next morning, a note and a small package were passed to Anne. The note read:

Dear Anne,

Mother says I'm not to play with you or talk to you even at school. It isn't my fault and don't be cross at me. I miss you so much and I don't like Gertie Pye one bit. I made you a bookmark out of red tissue paper. They are very fashionable now and only three girls in school know how to make them. When you look at it remember

Your true friend,

Diana Barry.

Anne replied back:

My Own Darling Diana,

Of course I'm not cross at you because you have to obey your mother. I shall keep your present forever. Minnie Andrews is a very nice girl though she has no imagination. But after having been your bosom friend, I can't be Minnie's.

Yours forever, Anne or Cordelia Shirley.

P.S. I shall sleep with your letter under my pillow tonight.

Chapter 11

Anne to the Rescue

Anne was devoted to her studies with all her heart and soul, determined to be the best in her class, but Gilbert Blythe seemed to have a similar plan as well.

The rivalry between them was soon apparent, and they tried to beat each other in every subject. Usually either one of them would be first in class.

At the end of the term, Anne and Gilbert were both promoted into the fifth class. They began to learn new subjects, and the hardest one for Anne was geometry.

"It's awful stuff, Marilla," Anne groaned. "Mr. Phillips says I'm terrible at it. And Gil—I mean, some of the others are so smart at it. Even Diana. Oh, I miss her so terribly."

One snowy January evening, Anne was studying at the kitchen table while Matthew was dozing off on the sofa. Marilla had gone to Charlottetown to attend the address given by the Canadian Premier.

Anne really wanted to read a novel. But if she did, Gilbert would beat her in geometry tomorrow.

All of a sudden, there came the sound of flying footsteps on the icy walk outside. The next moment the kitchen door was flung open and in rushed Diana Barry.

"Whatever is the matter, Diana?" cried Anna. "Has your mother forgiven me at last?"

"Oh, Anne, do come quick," begged Dianna. "Minnie May is awfully sick—she's got croup. Father and Mother are away in Charlottetown. They hired Mary Joe to look after us while they're gone, But Mary Joe doesn't know what to do. Oh, Anne, I'm so scared!"

Matthew, without a word, reached out for cap and coat. He slipped past Diana and went into the yard.

"He's gone to get the doctor," Anne said as she hurriedly put on her jacket.

"But all the doctors are probably in Charlottetown," sobbed Diana.

"Don't cry, Diana," Anne said. "I know exactly what to do. You forget that Mrs. Hammond had twins three times. They had croup all the time. Just wait till I get some medicine. You might not have any at your house."

The girls went out into the frosty night hand in hand and hurried over to Diana's house.

Minnie May, only three years old, was feverish. Her hoarse breathing could be heard all over the house.

"First, we must have lots of hot water. There, I've filled up the kettle. Mary Joe," said Anne, "you may put some wood in the stove. You might have thought of this if you'd any imagination."

Anne gave Minnie May some medicine. Then she undressed Minnie May and put her to bed.

Anne and Diana sat with Minnie May all night. Anne gave her every drop of medicine in the bottle.

It was three in the morning when Matthew came with a doctor. He had gone all the way to Spencervale to find one. But by then, Minnie May was much better and sleeping soundly. Anne was exhausted when she went home with Matthew.

Anne went to bed and didn't wake up until the afternoon. She dressed and went downstairs, finding Marilla knitting in the kitchen.

"Your lunch is in the oven," Marilla said. "And you can get yourself some plum preserve out of the pantry. I guess you're hungry. Matthew has told me about last night. Now, never mind talking till you've finished your food."

After Anne had finished her plums, Marilla said, "Mrs. Barry was here this afternoon, Anne. She wanted to see you, but I wouldn't wake you up. She says you saved Minnie May's life, and the doctor said so too. Also, she's very sorry she acted as she did about the currant wine. She knows now you didn't mean to get Diana drunk, and she hopes you'll forgive her and be good friends with Diana again. You're to go over there this afternoon, if you like."

Anne's face radiated with happiness.

"Oh, Marilla, can I go right now?" asked Anne. "I'll wash the dishes when I come back."

"Yes, yes, run along," Marilla said indulgently.

Anne dashed into the cold without even putting on her jacket.

Chapter 12

The First Sleepover

"Oh, Marilla," Anne said one February evening. "You know tomorrow is Diana's birthday. Her mother said I could stay all night with her. In the spare room! But first we're going to the school concert. Oh, please, can I go, Marilla?"

Finally, Marilla agreed.

The next evening, Anne and Diana drove to the concert in a big sleigh with Diana's cousins.

Anne enjoyed all the performances except for one that failed to interest her. When Gilbert recited his poem, Anne picked up a book and read it until he had finished.

It was late when the girls got home. Everyone seemed asleep, so Anne and Diana tiptoed into the parlor next to the spare room. Diana said, "Let's change in here. It's so nice and warm."

Afterwards, Anne suggested, "Let's race and see who'll get to the bed first."

The two girls flew down the parlor and passed the spare-room door. They bounced on the bed at the same moment. And then— something—moved beneath them. There was a gasp and a cry. A voice said: "Merciful goodness!"

Anne and Diana rushed out of the room and tiptoed upstairs. "Who—or—what was it?" whispered Anne.

"It was Anne Josephine," said Diana, gasping for laughter. "She's father's aunt from Charlottetown. She's seventy and very prim and proper. Well, we'll have to sleep with Minnie May—and she kicks!"

Miss Josephine Barry did not show up for breakfast the next morning. Anne hurried home after breakfast. In the late afternoon, she went down to Mrs. Lynde's on an errand.

"So you and Diana nearly frightened poor old Miss Barry to death last night?" said Mrs. Lynde. "Mrs. Barry told me that Miss Barry has a terrible temper. She wouldn't speak to Diana at all."

"It wasn't Diana's fault," said Anne. "It was mine. I suggested racing to see who would get into bed first."

"I knew it had to be your idea!" said Mrs. Lynde. "Well, it's made a lot of trouble. Old Miss Barry came out to stay for a month, but now she's leaving tomorrow. She had promised to pay for Diana's music lessons, but she's changed her mind. The Barrys must be very upset. Miss Barry is rich, and they'd like to keep on the good side of her."

Anne ran toward Diana's house, and Diana met her at the kitchen door.

"Your Aunt Josephine was very cross, wasn't she?" asked Anne. "Why didn't you tell them it was my fault?"

"I would never do that," Diana said. "I'm not a telltale, Anne. Anyhow, I was just as much to blame as you."

"Well, I'm going to tell her myself," said Anne. Then she walked up to the living room door and knocked.

"Come in," said a sharp voice.

Anne entered the room, and Miss Barry was sitting by the fire. She glared through her gold-rimmed glasses at Anne.

"Who are you?" demanded Miss Barry.

"I'm Anne of Green Gables, and I've come to confess, if you please."

"Confess what?" Miss Barry snapped.

"That it was all my fault about jumping into bed on you last night. I suggested it. So you mustn't blame Diana."

"Oh, I must? Diana did her share of the jumping!"

"But we were only playing around. I think you ought to forgive us. Anyhow, please forgive Diana and let her have her music lessons. If you must be cross, be cross with me."

"You don't know what it is to be awakened out of a sound sleep by two girls bouncing on you," the old lady stopped staring.

"It must have been terrible," said Anne. "But there's our side of it, too. We didn't know there was anybody in that bed and you nearly scared us to death, too. And we couldn't sleep in the spare room after being promised. I suppose you are used to sleeping in spare rooms. Just imagine what you would feel like if you were a little orphan girl who had never had such an honor."

Miss Barry started laughing and said, "I'm afraid my imagination is a little rusty. Sit down here and tell me about yourself."

"I'm very sorry I can't," said Anne firmly. "I have to go home. But before I go, I do wish you would forgive Diana and stay here."

Miss Barry smiled. "Maybe I will if you come over and talk to me sometimes."

That evening, Miss Barry told Diana's parents that she had unpacked her bag.

"I've made up my mind to stay so that I could get to know that Anne-girl," she said. "She amuses me."

Miss Barry stayed her month out and over. When she went away, she said, "Remember, you Anne-girl, when you come to town, you're to visit me. I'll put you in my very sparest spare-room to sleep."

Chapter 13

Anne Takes a Dare

Diana gave a party for the girls in her class. They decided to play a new game—daring.

Josie Pye was first.

"Jane Andrews," she said, "I dare you to hop on one leg around the garden without stopping."

Jane was defeated. She could only hop to the second corner of the garden.

Then Anne dared Josie Pye to walk along the top of the board fence, which Josie finished quickly and easily.

"I don't think it's such a great thing to walk a little, low, board fence," Anne said. "I knew a girl who could walk the top of a roof."

"I don't believe it," said Josie flatly. "I don't believe anybody could. YOU couldn't, anyhow."

"Couldn't I?" Anne shouted.

"Then I dare you to limp up there and walk on the top of Mr. Barry's kitchen roof!" said Josie.

Anne turned pale, but she walked toward the house, where a ladder was leaning against the kitchen roof. All the girls followed behind, surprised that Anne would actually do it. "Don't you do it, Anne," begged Diana. "You'll fall off and be killed"

"I must do it. My honor is at stake," said Anne solemnly. "If I am killed you are to have my pearl bead ring."

Anne climbed the ladder amid silence. She balanced herself on the rooftop and started to walk. First, she managed to take several steps.

Then she swayed, lost her balance, flailed and fell. Sliding down the roof, she crashed on the ground.

Diana and the other girls had rushed around the house to where she had fallen.

"Anne, are you killed?" shrieked Diana, kneeling down. "Oh, dear Anne, speak just one word to me!"

Anne sat dizzily up. "No, Diana. I am not killed, but I am unconscious."

"Where? Oh, where, Anne?" someone started sobbing.

Before Anne could answer, Mrs. Barry appeared. Anne tried to get up, but sank back again with a sharp cry of pain.

"What's the matter? Where have you hurt yourself?" asked Mrs. Barry.

"My ankle," gasped Anne. "I know I can't walk home. And I'm sure I couldn't hop back on one foot."

Marilla was out in the orchard when she saw Mr. Barry coming up the slope, carrying Anne.

At that moment Marilla realized how much she loved Anne. She knew that Anne was dearer to her than anything else on earth.

"Mr. Barry, what has happened to her?" she gasped.

Anne answered, lifting her head. "Don't be very frightened, Marilla. I was walking on top of the Barrys' roof and fell off. I think I have sprained my ankle. But let's look on the bright side. I might have broken my neck."

Marilla showed them to the kitchen and said, "Bring her in here, Mr. Barry, and lay her on the sofa. Mercy me, the child has fainted!"

Matthew hurried back from the harvest field and went to get the doctor, who concluded that Anne had broken her ankle.

That night, Marilla went up to the east gable, where Anne was lying in bed in a cast.

"Aren't you very sorry for me, Marilla?" Anne asked quietly.

"It was your own fault," said Marilla, pulling down the blind and lighting a lamp.

"But what would you have done, Marilla," said Anne, "if you had been dared to walk on the rooftop?"

"I'd have stayed on the ground and let them dare away. Such

nonsense!" said Marilla.

Anne sighed. "But you have such strength, Marilla. I haven't. I just felt that I had to take Josie Pye's dare. If I didn't, she would have bragged about it all my life. Please don't be mad at me. I won't be able to go around for six or seven weeks. And Gil—I mean, everybody will get ahead of me in class. But I'll try to bear it all bravely if only you won't be cross with me, Marilla."

"There, there, I'm not cross," said Marilla. " Here now, try and eat some supper."

During the seven weeks that followed, she had many visitors. Her friends brought her flowers and books and told her all the happenings at school.

"Everybody has been so kind, Marilla," sighed Anne happily. "Even Josie Pye came to see me. I think she was sorry she dared me to walk on the roof. Diana told me we've had a new teacher, Miss Muriel Stacey. Diana says she has lovely blond hair and blue eyes. Her sleeve puffs are bigger than anybody else's in Avonlea. Every Friday afternoon she has everyone recite poems or plays. Miss Stacy also takes them all to the woods to study plants and birds. I can't wait to go to school and I believe that Miss Stacy is a kindred spirit."

"There's one thing for certain, Anne," Marilla smiled and said, "and that is that your fall hasn't injured your tongue at all."

Chapter 14

A Merry Christmas

It was October again when Anne was ready to go back to school. In November, the students of Avonlea school began to plan a Christmas concert, which was Miss Stacy's idea. Anne was excited about it, but Marilla thought it was all foolishness.

"I don't approve of children in these concerts. It's just filling your heads up with nonsense and taking time away from learning your lessons," Marilla grumbled.

"But think of the good cause," said Anne. "The money will be raised for a school flag, Marilla."

"Fiddlesticks!" said Marilla. "All you want is to have a good time."

"Well, it's fun organizing a concert. Diana is to sing a solo. I'm in two plays. The boys are going to have a dialogue too. And I will have two recitations, Marilla. I just tremble when I think of it, but it's a nice thrilling kind of tremble. Oh, Marilla, I know you are not as enthusiastic about it as I am, but don't you hope your little Anne will shine?"

"All I hope is that you'll behave yourself," said Marilla. "I'll be glad when all this fuss is over and you'll be able to settle down."

Anne sighed and went to the back yard, where Matthew was splitting wood.

"Well now, I reckon it's going to be a pretty good concert. And I expect you'll do your part fine," he said, smiling at her. Anne smiled back at him, glad that she had come to talk to Matthew. He was such a sweet old man.

Matthew had come into the kitchen, one cold, gray December evening. He had sat down in the woodbox corner to take off his heavy boots. Anne and her friends were practicing for the concert in the sitting room, laughing and chattering. Matthew suddenly became conscious that Anne was not dressed like the other girls. He noticed the other girls were all dressed in brightly-colored dresses. He wondered why Marilla always kept Anne's so dark and plain. "I would give her a nice new dress for Christmas." Matthew decided to turn to Mrs. Lynde for help.

"Pick out a dress for you to give Anne? No problem. I believe a nice rich brown would just suit Anne. Well, I'll sew it up if you don't mind."

"Well now, I'm much obliged," said Matthew, "and— and—I dunno—but I'd like—I think they make the sleeves different now. If it wouldn't be asking too much I—I'd like them made in the new way."

"Puffs? Of course. Don't worry about it, Matthew. I'll make it up in the very latest fashion," said Mrs. Lynde.

On Christmas morning, Anne ran downstairs. "Merry Christmas, Marilla! Merry Christmas, Matthew!"

Matthew had unfolded the dress from its paper wrapping. "Why—why—Matthew, is that for me?" Anne asked.

Anne took the dress and looked at it. It was soft and silky, with a ruffle of lace at the neck. But the sleeves were puffed!

"That's a Christmas present for you, Anne," said Matthew. "Why—why—Anne, don't you like it?"

"Like it! Oh, Matthew!" Anne laid the dress over a chair. "Matthew, it's perfect. Oh, I can never thank you enough. Look at those sleeves!"

"Well, well, let us have breakfast," said Marilla. "I don't think you need the dress; but since Matthew has got it for you, see that you take good care of it. There's a hair ribbon Mrs. Lynde left for you. It's brown, to match the dress."

When breakfast was over Anne and Diana met at the bridge in the hollow.

"I've got something more for you from Aunt Josephine," said Diana, handing her a box.

Anne opened the box. Inside it was a card and a pair of the leather slippers with beaded toes and satin bows and glistening buckles. "Oh, Diana," said Anne, "this is the best Christmas ever!"

The Christmas concert was held in the evening and was a

pronounced success. When it was all over, she and Diana walked home together under a starry sky.

"Your recitations just brought down the house, Anne. That sad one was simply splendid. When you ran off the platform, one of your roses fell out of your hair. I saw Gilbert pick it up and put it in his pocket. That's so romantic. Aren't you pleased with that?"

"It's nothing to me what that person does," said Anne. "I simply never waste a thought on him, Diana."

Chapter 15

Gone was the Red Hair

Marilla walked home one late April evening and found no sign of Anne in the kitchen. Then, she went up to the east gable for a candle. She saw Anne lying on the bed, face downward among the pillows.

"Goodness gracious! Have you been asleep, Anne?" said Marilla in astonishment.

"No," Anne answered into her pillows.

"Are you sick then?" asked Marilla anxiously, going over to the bed.

"No. But please, Marilla, go away and don't look at me."

"Anne Shirley, whatever is the matter with you? What have you done? Get right up this minute and tell me!" said Marilla.

Anne got up. "Look at my hair, Marilla," she whispered.

Marilla lifted her candle and looked at Anne's hair. She exclaimed in surprise. "Anne Shirley, what have you done to your hair? Why, it's GREEN!"

"Yes, it's green," moaned Anne. "I thought nothing could be as bad as red hair. But now I know it's ten times worse to have green hair."

"What did you do to your hair?" asked Marilla.

"I dyed it."

"Dyed it! Dyed your hair! Anne Shirley, didn't you know it was a wicked thing to do?"

"Yes, I knew," admitted Anne. "But I thought it was worthwhile to get rid of my red hair. I bought the dye from a peddler this afternoon. He said it would turn my hair a beautiful raven black."

"Come right down to the kitchen to give your hair a good washing and see if that will do any good," said Marilla.

But the dye wouldn't wash off. For a week, Anne went nowhere and shampooed her hair every day, but it was still green.

Marilla said decidedly: "It's no use, Anne. Your hair must be cut off; there is no other way. You can't stay home from school anymore."

Marilla had cut her hair very short. Nobody teased Anne's clipped head in school except for Josie Pye.

"Josie said I look like a perfect scarecrow," Anne confided that evening to Marilla. "And I wanted to say something back. But I didn't. I just swept her one scornful look and then I forgave her. Am I talking too much, Marilla? Does it hurt your head?"

"My head is better now. As for your chatter, I don't mind it— I've got so used to it."

It was Marilla's way of saying that she liked to hear it.

Chapter 16

The Boating Incident

Anne, Diana, Ruby and Jane were standing on the bank of the Lake of the Shining Waters one midsummer afternoon. The girls were discussing who should play Elaine, the fair maiden, who died for the handsome knight, Sir Lancelot.

It was Anne's idea that they should act out the romantic story of Elaine. "After Elaine dies, she floats down to Camelot in a barge," said Anne. "Your father's boat could be used as the barge, Diana."

"You must be Elaine, Anne," said Diana. "I could never have the courage to float down there."

"Well, I'll be Elaine," said Anne, getting on to the boat. "Ruby, you must be King Arthur and Jane will be Guinevere and Diana must be Lancelot. Now, where do you go to meet up? Right, at Camelot, I mean, at the other side of the pond."

Anne lay down on the bottom of the boat, with closed eyes and hands folded over her breast.

"Now, she's all ready," Jane instructed the other girls. "Push the boat off."

They pushed, and the boat floated out into the current.

Anne drifted slowly down, enjoying dramatizing Elaine, the maiden who had loved Sir Lancelot. Suddenly, the boat began to leak. Anne scrambled to her feet and gazed at a big crack in the bottom of her boat through which the water was literally pouring. At this rate the boat would sink!

The boat drifted down to the log bridge and the water rose in it every moment. Then the boat bumped right into a pile made out of old tree trunks. Anne scrambled up on a big tree trunk, clinging on tight to it. The boat drifted under the bridge and then promptly sank in midstream.

Ruby, Jane, and Diana saw the boat disappear before their very eyes and thought Anne had gone down with it. They stood still, frozen with horror at the tragedy; then, shrieking at the tops of their voices, they started on a frantic run up through the woods, never pausing as they crossed the main road to glance the way of the bridge.

Anne saw their flying forms and heard their shrieks. "Please bring help soon," she whispered.

Anne was not sure how much longer she could hold on to that precarious stub. It felt like an eternity. "Why didn't somebody come?" Anne thought to herself.

Then, just as she thought she really could not endure the ache in her arms and wrists another moment, Gilbert Blythe came rowing under the bridge! Gilbert glanced up and, much to his amazement, beheld a little white scornful face looking down upon him with big, frightened but also scornful gray eyes.

He pulled close to the pile and extended his hand. Knowing she had no better options, Anne reluctantly clung to Gilbert Blythe's hand and scrambled down into the boat.

"What has happened, Anne?" asked Gilbert.

"We were playing Elaine" explained Anne frigidly, without even looking at him, "and I had to drift down to Camelot in the barge—I mean the boat. The boat began to leak and I climbed out on the pile. Will you be kind enough to row me to the landing?"

Gilbert rowed to the landing and Anne sprang onto the shore.

"Thank you very much," she said awkwardly as she turned away.

But Gilbert had also sprung from the boat and now took her arm.

"Anne," he said, "look here. Can't we be good friends? I'm awfully sorry I made fun of your hair that time. Besides, it's so long ago. I think your hair is very pretty now. Let's be friends." Gilbert looked eagerly into her eyes. Her heart gave a quick little beat.

But she remembered vividly how much he had hurt her feelings when he had called her 'carrots' and had brought about her disgrace before the whole school. She would never forgive him!

"No," she said coldly, "I shall never be friends with you, Gilbert Blythe!"

"All right!" Gilbert sprang into his boat. "I'll never ask you to be friends again, Anne Shirley."

He pulled away, and Anne held her head very high, but she was conscious of an odd feeling of regret. She wished she had forgiven Gilbert this time around.

Halfway up the path she met Jane and Diana rushing back to the pond. "Oh, Anne," gasped Diana. "We thought—you were—drowned. Oh, Anne, how did you escape?"

"I climbed up on one of the piles," explained Anne wearily, "and Gilbert Blythe came along and brought me to land."

"Oh, Anne, it's so romantic!" said Jane. "Of course you'll speak to him after this."

"Of course I won't," said Anne.

Anne told Marilla later that day, "I'm going to stop being too romantic. I thought it would be romantic to dye my hair black and play Elaine. Instead, my hair turned out to be green and I nearly drowned. I think my prospects of becoming sensible are brighter now than ever and I'll stay out of trouble. I feel quite sure that you will soon see a great improvement in me in this respect, Marilla."

"I'm sure I hope so," said Marilla skeptically.

Chapter 17

The Big Exam

"Anne," said Marilla one night in November, "Miss Stacy was here this afternoon."

Anne was curled up on the hearthrug, gazing into the fire. She looked up at Marilla with a start.

"Oh, I'm so sorry I wasn't in. Why was Miss Stacy here this afternoon?" asked Anne.

"Well, Miss Stacy wants to organize a class to study for the entrance examination into Queen's. And she came to ask Matthew and me if we would like to have you join it. What do you think about it yourself, Anne? Would you like to go to Queen's and pass for a teacher?"

"Oh, Marilla!" Anne said. "I'd love to be a teacher. But won't it be dreadfully expensive?"

"You needn't worry about that part of it," said Marilla. "Matthew and I resolved we would save up some money for you and give you a good education."

"Oh, Marilla, thank you." Anne flung her arms about Marilla's waist. "I'll study as hard as I can and do my very best to make you proud of me."

The Queen's class was organized in due time. Gilbert Blythe, Anne Shirley, Ruby Gillis, Jane Andrews, and Josie Pye joined it. They stayed after class every day to study for the entrance exam.

The open rivalry between Gilbert and Anne was rather strong now. Gilbert was as determined as Anne to be first in class. Gilbert talked and joked with the other girls, and sometimes walked home with them. But Anne Shirley he simply ignored.

Anne found out that it is not pleasant to be ignored. Deep down, she knew that she was responsible for this predicament. She found that the old resentment against him was gone. Anne realized that she had forgiven and forgotten without knowing it. But it was too late.

When the term ended, Anne stacked all her textbooks away in an old trunk in the attic, locked it, and threw the key into the blanket box.

"I'm not even going to look at a schoolbook in vacation," she told Marilla. "I've studied as hard all the term as I possibly could. I want to have a real good time this summer."

In September, Anne went back to Avonlea school, recharged and eager to work hard once more.

One day, Marilla was astonished to find Anne, who turned fifteen that March, was taller than herself. And that night, Matthew caught Marilla sat alone and indulged in the weakness of a cry. He gazed at her with concern since Marilla hardly ever cried!

"I was thinking about Anne," she explained. "She's grown to be such a big girl—and she'll probably be away from us next winter. I'll miss her terribly."

"She'll be able to come home often," comforted Matthew.

"It won't be the same thing as having her here all the time," sighed Marilla gloomily.

Anne was looking forward to studying at Queen's, but she had to pass the entrance exam first.

In June, Anne and her classmates went to Charlottetown for the entrance exam, and Anne stayed with Aunt Josephine for a week while she was in town.

Anne arrived home on Friday evening, rather tired but with an air of chastened triumph about her.

"I think I did pretty well in everything except for geometry. I have a creepy feeling that I didn't pass."

"Oh, you'll pass all right. Don't worry."

In fact, Anne's goal was more than just passing the exam. To her, success would be incomplete and bitter if she did not come out ahead of Gilbert Blythe. Also, she wanted to 'pass high' for Matthew and Marilla—to make them proud of her achievement.

Still, three weeks had gone by without the pass list appearing.

But one evening, Anne was sitting at her open window, when she saw Diana come flying down toward Green Gables with a fluttering newspaper in her hand. Diana burst into the room without even knocking, so great was her excitement.

"Anne, you've passed," she cried, "passed the VERY FIRST—you and Gilbert both—you're ties—but your name is first. Oh, I'm so proud!"

"I'm just dazzled inside," said Anne. "I've dreamed of coming out first on the pass list, but I never thought it would actually come true!"

Chapter 18

The Scholarship

In fall, Anne started classes at Queen's Academy, and Aunt Josephine helped her find a boarding house. Homesickness seized upon Anne at first. Fortunately, she's got Jane and Ruby, and she didn't even mind Josie Pye's companionship.

Anne's homesickness wore off, greatly helped in the wearing by her weekend visits home and a circle of new friends at the Academy. Anne resolved to study hard and steadily to win a scholarship to Redmond College. There were two kinds of scholarships: the Medal and the Avery.

"I have no hope of winning the Avery," said Anne to Jane after the final exams and before the results were announced. "Everybody says Emily Clay will win it. And I'm not going to march up to that bulletin board and look at it before everybody. You must read the announcements and then come and tell me. If I have failed, break it gently. Promise me this, Jane."

Jane promised solemnly. However, when they went up the entrance steps of Queen's they found the hall full of boys who were carrying Gilbert Blythe around on their shoulders and yelling at the tops of their voices, "Hurrah for Blythe, Medalist!"

For a moment Anne felt one sickening pang of defeat and disappointment. So she had failed and Gilbert had won! Well,

Matthew would be sorry—he had been so sure she would win.

And then! Somebody called out: "Three cheers for Miss Shirley, winner of the Avery!"

And then the girls were around them and Anne was the center of a laughing, congratulating group. Anne whispered to Jane: "Oh, won't Matthew and Marilla be pleased!"

Commencement was held in the big assembly hall of the Academy. Matthew and Marilla were there watching Anne read the best essay and was pointed out and whispered about as the Avery winner.

"Reckon you're glad we kept her, Marilla?" whispered Matthew.

"It's not the first time I've been glad," retorted Marilla. "You do like to rub things in, Matthew Cuthbert."

Anne went home to Avonlea with Matthew and Marilla that evening. Diana was at Green Gables to meet her.

"Oh, Diana, it's so good to be back again. And it's GOOD to see you again, Diana!"

"You've done splendidly, Anne. Will you be teaching now that you've won the Avery?"

"No. I'm going to Redmond in September. Doesn't it seem wonderful? But first I'll have three glorious, golden months of vacation."

The next morning at breakfast it suddenly struck Anne that Matthew was not looking well. "Marilla," she said hesitatingly, "is Matthew quite well?"

"No, he isn't," said Marilla in a troubled tone. "He's had some real bad spells with his heart this spring and he won't spare himself. I've been really worried about him. I'm hoping he'll kind of rest and pick up now that you're home. You always cheer him up."

In the evening she went with Matthew to bring the cows to the back pasture.

"You've been working too hard today, Matthew," she said. "Why won't you take things easier?"

"Well now, it's only that I'm getting old, Anne, and keep forgetting it," said Matthew.

"If I had been the boy you sent for," said Anne wistfully, "I'd be able to help you so much now and spare you in a hundred ways. I could find it in my heart to wish I had been, just for that."

"Well now, I'd rather have you than a dozen boys, Anne," said Matthew, patting her hand. "Just mind you that— rather than a dozen boys. Well now, I guess it wasn't a boy that took the Avery scholarship, was it? It was a girl—my girl—my girl that I'm proud of."

Chapter 19

Hard Times

"Matthew—Matthew—what is the matter? Matthew, are you sick?"Marilla called out.

Anne hurried toward the kitchen. They were both too late; before they could reach him Matthew had fallen to the floor.

"Anne, run for Martin— quick, quick!" Martin, the hired man, started at once for the doctor. But it was too late. Matthew had passed away.

In the night, Marilla heard Anne crying and went into her room to comfort her. "There—there—don't cry so, dear. It can't bring him back."

"Oh, Marilla, what will we do without him?" sobbed Anne.

"We've got each other, Anne. I don't know what I'd do if you weren't here—if you'd never come. Oh, Anne, I know I've been kind of strict and harsh with you maybe— but you mustn't think I didn't love you as well as Matthew did, for all that. I love you as dear as if you were my own flesh and blood and you've been my joy and comfort ever since you came to Green Gables."

Two days afterwards they buried Matthew. And then Avonlea settled back to its usual placidity. Anne, new to grief, thought about Matthew often.

One evening, Marilla was sitting on the front doorsteps and Anne sat down beside her.

"Doctor Spencer was here while you were away," Marilla said. "He says that the specialist will be in town tomorrow and he insists that I must go in and have my eyes examined. I'll be more than thankful if the man can give me the right kind of glasses to suit my eyes. You won't mind staying here alone while I'm away, will you?"

"I shall be all right. Diana will come over to keep me company. You needn't fear that I'll get into any new trouble."

Marilla laughed. "Do you remember the time you dyed your hair?"

"Yes, indeed. I shall never forget it," smiled Anne. "I did suffer terribly over my hair and my freckles. My freckles are really gone; and people are nice enough to tell me my hair is auburn now—all but Josie Pye."

Marilla went to town the next day and returned in the evening. Sitting by the table, she leaned her head on her hand.

"Are you very tired, Marilla?" Anne asked.

"It's not that," said Marilla wearily. "The eye doctor examined my eyes. He says that if I give up all reading and sewing entirely and any kind of work that strains the eyes, my eyes may not get any worse and my headaches will be cured. But if I don't, he says I'll certainly be blind in six months."

"If you are careful you won't lose your sight altogether; and if his glasses cure your headaches it will be a great thing."

"What am I to live for if I can't read or sew or do anything like that?" said Marilla bitterly. "I might as well be blind."

When Marilla had gone to bed, Anne went herself to the east gable and sat down by her window. She thought about how to help Marilla with her predicament. Before long, she had figured out a solution.

Chapter 20

The Dear Old Green Gables

A few days later, Anne saw Marilla talking to a man at the front yard. There were tears in her eyes and her voice broke as she said, "He heard that I was going to sell Green Gables and he wants to buy it."

"Buy it! Buy Green Gables?" Anne was surprised.

"Anne, I don't know what else is to be done. I've thought it all over. I may lose my sight altogether; and anyway I'll not be fit to run things. Oh, I never thought I'd live to see the day when I'd have to sell my home." Marilla broke down and wept bitterly.

"You mustn't sell Green Gables," said Anne resolutely.

"Oh, Anne, I wish I didn't have to. But you can see for yourself. I can't stay here alone."

"You won't have to stay here alone, Marilla. I'll be with you. I'm not going to Redmond."

"Not going to Redmond!" Marilla lifted her worn face from her hands and looked at Anne.

"Just what I say. I'm not going to take the scholarship. I decided so the night after you came home from town. You surely don't think I could leave you alone in your trouble, Marilla, after all you've done for me."

"Let me tell you my plans. Mr. Barry wants to rent the farm for next year. So you won't have any bother over that. And I'm going to teach. I've applied for the Avonlea school here—but I don't expect to get it for I understand the trustees have promised it to Gilbert Blythe. But I can teach at the Carmody school. I can board home and drive myself over to Carmody and back. And I'll read to you and keep you cheered up after work."

"But don't you want to go to Redmond?"

"There is no sacrifice. Nothing could be worse than giving up Green Gables— nothing could hurt me more. We must keep the dear old place. My mind is quite made up, Marilla. I'm NOT going to Redmond; and I AM going to stay here and teach. I mean to study at home here and take a little college course all by myself. Taking care of dear Green Gables and you are of the utmost importance right now."

"I guess I ought to stick out and make you go to college—but I know I can't, so I ain't going to try. I'll make it up to you though, Anne."

Mrs. Lynde came up one evening and told Anne and Marilla, "The trustees have decided to give you the Avonlea school to teach."

"Why, I thought they had promised it to Gilbert Blythe!"

"So they did. But as soon as Gilbert heard that you had

applied for it he went to them and told them that he withdrew his application, and suggested that they accept yours. He said he was going to teach at White Sands. Of course he knew how much you wanted to stay with Marilla."

"I don't feel that I ought to take it. I don't think I ought to let Gilbert make such a sacrifice for—for me."

"I guess you can't prevent him now. He's signed papers with the White Sands trustees. So it wouldn't do him any good now if you were to refuse. Of course you'll take the school."

Anne went to the little Avonlea graveyard the next evening to put fresh flowers on Matthew's grave. When she was on the way home, she bumped into Gilbert. He lifted his cap courteously, but he would have passed on in silence, if Anne had not stopped and held out her hand.

"Gilbert," she said, with scarlet cheeks, "I want to thank you for giving up the school for me. It was very good of you—and I want you to know that I appreciate it."

Gilbert took the offered hand eagerly. "I was pleased to be able to do you some small service. Are we going to be friends after this? Have you really forgiven me for my old fault?"

Anne laughed. "I forgave you that day by the pond landing, although I didn't know it. I've been sorry ever since."

"We are going to be the best of friends," said Gilbert, jubilantly. "We were born to be good friends, Anne. Come, I'm going to walk home with you."

Marilla looked curiously at Anne when the latter entered the kitchen. "Who was it that came up the lane with you, Anne?"

"Gilbert Blythe. I met him on Barry's hill."

"I didn't think you and Gilbert Blythe were such good friends that you'd stand for half an hour at the gate talking to him," said Marilla with a dry smile.

"Were we really there for half an hour? It seemed like just a few minutes. But, you see, we have five years' lost conversations to catch up with, Marilla."

Anne sat long at her window that night accompanied by a glad content. The wind purred softly in the cherry boughs and the apple tree branches. The stars twinkled over the pointed firs in the hollow and Diana's light gleamed through the old gap.

Anne looked forward to the exciting future. She would be a teacher, keep up her studies, and enjoy all the friendship she's built up over the years.

Best of all, she knew that the old Green Gables would always be her sweet home.

◆團隊簡介◆

計畫主編｜陳麗君

新營人。國立成功大學台文系所副教授，兼任新聞中心主任、性別 kah 婦女研究中心研究員、《台灣語文研究》執行編輯等。長期 tshui-sak 台灣各族群（原住民、台語、新住民）社會語言學研究 kah 活動。最近發表新冊《新移民、女性、母語 ê 社會語言學》（2021）。

台文譯者｜黃昭瑞

高雄原生種。國立臺南女中英文教師。原底台語無 liàn 轉，有身期間智覺 tiòh 台灣各種語言 lóng 強 beh 絕種去，就決定 beh kah gín-á 講台語。十二年來 kā 華、英語故事口譯做台語故事，建立規家伙 á ê 台語基礎。Bat 擔任葫蘆巷讀冊協會理事，期間 tī 新樓幼兒園 hām 市立圖書館講台語故事，鼓勵爸母 kah gín-á 講母語。

台文譯者兼校對｜白麗芬

彰化人。教育部、成大台語認證專業級。104 年全國語文競賽閩南語字音字形社會組第一名。金安出版社《咱來考 C》、《臺語活詞典首冊》編輯委員，全國語文競賽閩南語朗讀稿作者。Bat 擔任語文競賽講師、評審，台語認證研習講師。作品散見《台文罔報》、《海翁台語文學》、《台客詩刊》、《臺江臺語文學季刊》等。

英文校對 │ 蘇凰蘭

美國 Illinois University at Urbana-Champaign 東亞語言文化博士。國立臺東大學華語文學系副教授。學術興趣是母語教育、雙語讀寫、語言學習動機 kap hānn 語言實踐。

插畫 │ Asta Wu 吳雅怡

現此時是專職 ê 插畫家，畫插圖、畫繪本 mā 畫圖像小說，啖試各種創作 ê 方式，目前 tng-leh 往寫故事 ê 方向伐進。佮意神話、民俗傳說 kah 貓咪，上愛 tī 作品內底藏小動物 kah tsē-tsē 無 kâng 款式 ê 彩卵。（astawu.com　IG：Asta Wu）

台文校對兼錄音指導 │ 林月娥

嘉義水上人。成大台文所碩士，成大 kah 教育部台語認證 C2 專業級。國立屏東大學台語課程講師 kah 語文競賽評委；高雄市台語認證研習講師；95 年全國語文競賽台語即席演說 kah 97 年台語朗讀第一名，102 年教育部閩客語文學獎教師組現代詩第二名 kah 107 年屏東縣閩客原文學獎散文社會組第一名。詩文散見《海翁台語文學》、《教育部電子報》、高雄歷史博物館 ê「高雄小故事」。

有聲朗讀（說書 kap 姑婆等）│ 林月娥

台語是阮 ê 枕頭伴，上愛用好聽 ê 聲音，講上媠 ê 台語！

有聲朗讀（安妮）| 陳宥蓁 (14 歲)

屏東縣屏東市中正國中。上愛跳舞，台語、客語雙聲帶，語文競賽定定 tióh 頭名。

有聲朗讀（馬修 等男聲）| 許廷安 (12 歲)

屏東縣屏東市中正國中。中正國小畢業 tióh 縣長獎，堅持用台語講出對老師 kah 對阿母 ê 感謝。

有聲朗讀（瑪俐 kap 黛娜）| 潘韵弦 (11 歲)

屏東縣屏東市中正國小。阿母講：認真讀冊 tsiok 要緊，台語講會 láu 愈 gâu！

有聲朗讀（萊義柏 等男聲）| 張胤玄 (11 歲)

屏東縣屏東市中正國小。愛拍鼓、gâu 畫圖，108 年全國美術比賽（漫畫類）tióh 特優，gâu 講台語，tióh 過第一屆番薯電視台本土文化獎講古比賽第三名。

編輯助理 | 高于棋

成大台文大二 ê 學生。Bat 擔任校刊 ê 主編、《中市青年》專欄。Bat tióh 中台灣聯合文學獎新詩組首獎、全球華文青年文學獎散文組入圍等獎項。

國家圖書館出版品預行編目 (CIP) 資料

青瓦厝 ê 安妮 /Lucy Maud Montgomery 原著；黃昭瑞，
白麗芬譯 . -- 初版 . -- 臺北市：前衛出版社 , 2022.02
　面；　公分
台英對照
ISBN 978-626-7076-12-5(精裝)

885.3596　　　　　　　　　　　　　110022296

世界文學台讀少年雙語系列・2・

青瓦厝 ê 安妮（台英雙語・附台語朗讀）

原　　著　Lucy Maud Montgomery
譯　　者　黃昭瑞、白麗芬
主　　編　陳麗君
編輯助理　高于棋
插　　畫　Asta Wu（吳雅怡）
台文校對　林月娥、白麗芬
英文校對　蘇鳳蘭
美術設計　鄭惠敏、線在創作設計工作室 / Sunline Design
朗讀指導　林月娥
有聲朗讀　林月娥、陳宥蓁、許廷安、潘韵弦、張胤玄
錄音混音　音樂人多媒體工作室
出版贊助　天母扶輪社、北區扶輪社、明德扶輪社
　　　　　至善扶輪社、天和扶輪社、天欣扶輪社

出 版 者　前衛出版社
　　　　　地址：104056 台北市中山區農安街 153 號 4 樓之 3
　　　　　電話：02-25865708 ｜傳真：02-25863758
　　　　　郵撥帳號：05625551
　　　　　購書・業務信箱：a4791@ms15.hinet.net
　　　　　投稿・代理信箱：avanguardbook@gmail.com
　　　　　官方網站：http://www.avanguard.com.tw

出版總監　林文欽
法律顧問　陽光百合律師事務所
總 經 銷　紅螞蟻圖書有限公司
　　　　　地址：114066 台北市內湖區舊宗路二段 121 巷 19 號
　　　　　電話：02-27953656 ｜傳真：02-27954100
出版日期　2022 年 2 月初版一刷｜2023 年 12 月初版二刷
定　　價　新台幣 450 元